COLLECTED STORIES

DON TASSONE

Contents

Sorrow

Joy

Toerner Press
3395 St. George's Way
Loveland, OH 45140

Print ISBN: 978-0-578-35435-4

Cover design by Tim Poirier

For Alice

Author's Note

Most of the stories in this book have been featured in the author's previous short story collections.

Acknowledgements

I want to thank my wife Liz for her abiding support, Libby Belle for suggesting this collection and Tim Poirier for designing the cover.

I also want to extend grateful acknowledgment to the editors of the online literary magazines where the original versions of many of these stories appeared: *Friday Flash Fiction, Red Fez, The Zodiac Review, TWJ Magazine, The Story Shack, 101 Words, Down in the Dirt Magazine, Ray's Road Review, formercactus, Flash Fiction Magazine, Page & Spine, Olentangy Review, Free Flash Fiction, Sick Lit Magazine, Edify Fiction, The Rush, Daily Science Fiction, Bright Flash Literary Review* and *Scarlet Leaf Review.*

Don Tassone

Preface

When a writing friend suggested putting this story collection together, I was initially hesitant, in part because *Collected Stories by Don Tassone* sounds like I'm dead.

But then one day I was with my beautiful goddaughter Alice. She is one of my nine wonderful grandchildren. Alice is four years old. She has Down syndrome.

When I look at Alice, I am reminded of why I write. I write as an invitation to appreciate life more deeply. Alice helps me appreciate life more deeply.

I am dedicating this book to Alice and giving the proceeds to the National Down Syndrome Society, the leading human rights organization for those who, like Alice, have been given an extra chromosome.

I've selected 50 favorite stories for this collection and organized them by five themes. Four stories — "Flashpoint", "Theo", "Show Me" and "Communion" — are nonfiction.

I hope you enjoy them all.

Don Tassone

March 2022

Blessing

Dorothy

I took my groceries from my cart and placed them on the belt.

I watched a young woman bagging groceries. She was short. Her face was flat, and her head was small. Her eyes were shaped like almonds. Her name tag said Dorothy.

When I was growing up, there was a boy in our neighborhood who looked like this. I never knew his name.

As the cashier scanned my items, I stepped forward to the bagging area.

"May I help you, Dorothy?"

"Sure," she said with a smile.

We stood there, Dorothy and I, side by side, bagging groceries together.

Beauty Mark

Claire Wilson had never been so happy. Two days earlier, she had graduated from high school. The following day, she signed a contract with a top modeling agency in New York City. She would start in two weeks.

She was all set to take a train with her parents to New York that weekend to find a place to live. Her lifelong dream of becoming a model was about to come true.

Now, as she was stepping out of the shower, Claire slipped on the wet tile floor. She fell so fast that she had no time to grab onto anything. The right side of her face hit the laminated corner of the sink, tearing a deep gash from her jawline to her hairline. The impact knocked her sideways. She hit the wall hard.

In the kitchen, her mother heard a thud, then Claire cry out. She rushed to the bathroom and found her daughter lying naked on the floor, her face covered with blood.

* * *

Claire had been such a beautiful baby — curly blond hair, powder blue eyes, charming dimples. She looked like she belonged on a package of Pampers.

As she grew older, Claire grew even lovelier. In grade school, all the girls wanted to look like her. In high school, all the boys wanted to be with her. On the street or in stores, she caught the eyes of many a passerby. Some would even stop and stare.

Claire enjoyed being the center of attention. It made her feel special. She loved hearing people say, “You should be a model.” As a girl, she had been drawn to the glamorous women in the ads in her mother’s magazines. She dreamed of being on a magazine cover one day.

When Claire was a teenager, her mother arranged for her to be professionally photographed. She sent her photos to the top modeling agencies in New York. By the time she graduated from high school, Claire had her pick of agencies. They’d been jockeying for her.

The day after she graduated, Claire chose the largest agency. She was impressed by their claim that their models had appeared on more fashion magazine covers than those from all the other top agencies combined.

They’d offered Claire a generous contract. She had just signed it and come home from the post office when she decided to take a shower.

Claire’s injury required more than 100 stitches. The emergency room surgeon closed the gaping wound, but the damage to her face was extensive. It would take a series of operations to advance the healing process.

The cost of the first two of those surgeries, to reconnect muscle and nerves, would be covered by the talent agency’s medical insurance.

After that, the surgeries would be considered cosmetic, and they weren't covered by the agency's policy. Hopeful that Claire might still have a shot at modeling, her parents dipped into their savings to cover the expense.

During the next four months, Claire underwent several more procedures. Fortunately, her doctors were successful in repairing much of the damage to her face. Only a faint scar remained. Unfortunately, it was slightly raised and noticeable, even with makeup. After reviewing new photos of Claire's face, the talent agency chose to exercise an escape clause in her contract.

The agency was merely confirming what Claire had known from the moment her head hit that sink, that her career in modeling — her dream — was over.

* * *

Yet Claire did not accept her fate easily.

"Why has this happened to me?" she sobbed to her mother.

"Claire, honey, I don't know. I'm so sorry."

"I've only ever wanted to be a model."

"I know, honey."

"Well, what I am supposed to do now?"

"Claire, you're so talented. You have a lot of other options."

"Like what, Mom?"

"Well, what are your other interests?"

"Mom! I have no other interests!"

Claire pounded her fists on the arms of the recliner she was sitting in and lurched forward, slamming the footrest into the base of the chair. She sprung to her feet and stomped across the family room and into the kitchen.

Her mother heard car keys scraping against a wooden board on the wall next to the door to the garage.

"Where you are going, honey?"

"Out!" Claire snapped, slamming the door behind her.

She got in her mom's car, pulled out of the driveway and sped down the street.

She drove through the streets of her small town, the only place she'd ever lived. She drove past her grade school, where she'd been crowned the May Queen, and her high school, where she'd been crowned Homecoming queen. These were among the happiest moments of her life. She wondered if she could ever be happy again.

Claire threw temper tantrums all that summer. Her parents tried to console her, saying her face was looking better all the time. That was true, but it wasn't what Claire wanted to hear. She wanted someone to tell her she should be a model again.

The attention she had always enjoyed, even craved, she now avoided. She now hated bumping into people she knew. That summer, she ran into Mrs. Adkins, a neighbor, in the grocery store.

"Claire!" she called. "How are you?"

Claire could feel the woman's eyes on her face.

"Good, Mrs. Adkins. I'm good."

"I was so sorry to hear about your accident."

"Thank you."

"You know, your injury is hardly noticeable now," Mrs. Adkins said, trying not to stare.

"Thank you."

Claire knew Mrs. Adkins was lying. She knew she was scarred for life. She knew her lifelong dream was dead.

* * *

That fall, as her friends left for college, Claire fell into a pattern of driving her mother's car aimlessly through the streets.

She drove past her favorite stores, friends' houses, the photography studio where she'd posed for modeling agency shots, her old schools, her church. These places made up the only world Claire had ever known.

But she had begun to long for something more. One day, she drove to the edge of town and kept driving. She came to a small college. She'd never been there. She drove slowly through the tree-lined streets, watching students stroll along the sidewalks.

A large, red-brick building with a round portico supported by white columns caught her eye. She was so struck by its elegance that she felt compelled to stop. She pulled into the parking lot.

Claire got out and walked up to the building. As she got near it, she could see some of the bricks were cracked, a good deal of the mortar was broken and the paint was chipped.

The building had looked so perfect from the street. Now, close up, Claire realized it was no less beautiful. In fact, its imperfections made it more interesting.

She followed a sidewalk toward the center of campus. Students passing by smiled and said hello. Claire felt welcome there. She began to feel good about herself again.

She found the admissions office, went inside and applied for enrollment in the spring.

* * *

In her sophomore year, Claire declared psychology as her major. She ended up with both a master's degree and a doctorate in psychology. Her dissertation was on "redefining beauty."

“We all tend to see ourselves as imperfect,” she wrote. “‘If only I could fix this one thing,’ we say to ourselves. But sometimes what we first see as a flaw we come to realize is a beauty mark. It allows us to see our real beauty, our truest beauty, in a way we might otherwise never know.”

Claire started giving talks to high school girls on this theme. She shared her own journey. She helped every girl she spoke to feel beautiful.

Glamour magazine heard about Claire’s talks. They did a feature story and put her on the cover.

Morning Prayer

He wakes up at six every morning even though he no longer sets an alarm. He makes a cup of black coffee, which he sips in a wide armchair under the soft glow of an old floor lamp.

He looks out into the darkness. Sometimes he sees stars, sometimes the moon. But he always sees faces, the faces of his loved ones, his old friends and strangers from the day before.

He says a prayer of thanks for each of them, and his lonely heart is soothed as the loving sun rises, and that's how he begins his day.

Presence

Jacob's fifth-grade classmates were thinking about him when he wasn't in school after his mother died, but they didn't know how or even whether to reach out.

Jacob had always been a "mama's boy." Now, without his mother, he felt so alone.

One day after school his friend Chloe came over. She lived a few doors down.

"Jake!" his father called upstairs. "Chloe's here for you."

She was standing in the foyer when he came down.

"Hi," she said.

"Hi," he said.

Neither of them knew quite what else to say and, at 11, hugging seemed too awkward.

"Want to swing?" she asked.

"Okay," he said.

She followed him into his backyard. They walked through the grass to his swing set and slipped into the yellow rubber swings, as they had countless times as children. When they were small, their mothers pushed them on these swings.

"Higher!" they would scream, laughing with delight and holding on tight. "Higher!"

Now they said nothing. They simply glided back and forth, like pendulums. Jacob felt as though he were suspended between two worlds, the one he had known and some other world where he would never feel his mother's loving touch again.

After a few minutes, Jacob slowed to a stop and Chloe did too. He stood up, shading his eyes from the late afternoon sun and hiding his tears.

A mourning dove flew in low overhead. It landed gracefully on the peak of the swing set and perched there.

"I love you" was the last thing Jacob's mother had said to him. Then she closed her eyes, and she never opened them again. He wondered if her words might still be in the air, hovering like a spirit above her bed.

"I need to go in," he said.

"Okay," said Chloe.

He started walking back to his house. She followed him, then veered into the side yard to let herself out through a wooden gate, as she had many times before.

Jacob stopped on his patio and looked over at her. Chloe was his oldest friend. He had known her long before his mother died, and he hoped he would know her long after. That idea, her coming over that afternoon, her being at the gate just then gave him comfort.

"Thanks," he said.

"Take care," she said.

At the BMV

"Next," said the middle-aged man sitting behind the counter at the Bureau of Motor Vehicles.

His voice was robotic. He didn't look up. He was staring at a computer screen. His eyes looked dead.

I understood. The BMV was probably my least favorite place in the world. I never imagined renewing my driver's license would be the highlight of my day.

I wondered if I could still pass the vision test. I wondered if this would be my last driver's license.

The line inched forward. The linoleum floor was wet from people tracking in snow. As I stepped forward, I slipped and fell down hard, landing on my back. My head hit the floor, and I nearly blacked out.

Those near me backed away. Maybe they were afraid of losing their places in line. Then, looking up, I saw the man who had been sitting behind the counter. He was now kneeling beside me.

"Are you okay, sir?" he said.

I moaned. I couldn't speak.

"Someone call 911," the man shouted.

He took off his sweater and balled it up. Then he gently lifted my head and slipped his sweater under it. It felt like a pillow.

I looked into his face. I saw concern in his eyes. It was the closest I had been to anyone, face to face, in years. I'd nearly forgotten what it was like to look into someone's eyes.

"I'll stay right here until help arrives," he said, patting my shoulder.

I noticed movement. People in line were moving forward around me. As they passed, they looked down at me with curious eyes.

When the EMTs got there, they checked me out, then lifted me onto a stretcher. The man from behind the counter helped them lift me. Then he picked up his sweater, stretched it out and carefully laid it on top of the blanket over me.

"Be well, sir," he said as they rolled me out.

On the way to the hospital, I wondered if the man had gone back to work. I wondered if his eyes had changed. I wondered if mine had changed.

Carousel

I found myself standing on a spinning carousel, holding onto a twisted brass pole. A panoply of images encircled me, people and experiences from throughout my life.

I watched them all pass by: every friend and enemy, every success and failure, every joy and sorrow. They all blended together.

I wanted to stop and behold the miracle of my daughter being born again. I wanted to unsee my mother dying. But I couldn't stop or close my eyes or pick and choose.

It was all my life, every part indispensable, and as I held on tight and looked around, I felt grateful for the whole of it.

Hold On

He drove a dark blue 1938 Buick Roadmaster. I wouldn't have known the year, the make or the model if my parents hadn't told me.

It was a relic. Whenever I saw it rolling down our street, I half expected gangsters to be hanging out of the windows, brandishing tommy guns. It didn't even sound like any other car on the road. All the cars I knew hummed or revved. This one clicked, like an egg timer.

But its driver seemed even more ancient and mysterious. We knew him only as Old Man Hopkins. None of us had ever met him. Even our parents called him Old Man Hopkins.

He lived at the end of our street in a house that was much older than all the others in our neighborhood. Once in a while, I would see him driving by. Maybe it was those small car windows. But I never got a good look at him. This, of course, only added to the mystery.

* * *

In the summer of 1970, when I was 12, I decided to make as much money as I could by cutting grass. I went door to door looking for customers.

Old Man Hopkins' yard was huge, and it was a mess. One morning, I rode my bike down to the end of our street. I walked up Old Man Hopkins' long gravel driveway and climbed the steps to his front porch. I took a deep breath and knocked on his door.

The door opened. I could barely see him through the outer screen door. He looked smaller and even older than I expected.

"Yes?"

"Mr. Hopkins?"

"Yes?"

"My name is Bill. I live down the street. I was wondering if you might need someone to cut your grass."

"Do you mean you?"

"Yes."

"How much do you charge?"

"Three dollars."

"I have a pretty big yard."

"That's okay. I can handle it."

"I'll give you five. When can you cut it?"

"This afternoon," I stammered.

"Deal. I'll be here. Come see me when you're done."

I had never cut a yard so big. It took three hours and two tanks of gas. When I was finished, I knocked on the old man's front door. He stepped out on the porch and looked around.

"Nice job," he said with a smile.

“Thanks.”

“I think you’ve earned a little more than five dollars today,” he said, handing me a twenty. “That should cover your gas too.”

“Thank you!”

“You’re welcome. You thirsty?”

“Yeah.”

“Hang on. I’ll be right back.”

In a minute, he came back out with a cold, eight-ounce bottle of Coke.

“Here you go.”

“Thanks.”

I was parched. I felt like chugging the Coke, but I didn’t think that would be polite. Still, I drank it down pretty fast.

“Can you cut my grass again next week?”

“Sure. What day is best?”

“Whatever works for you. I’m here all the time. Just knock when you’re done, and we’ll settle up.”

“Sounds great. Thanks again, Mr. Hopkins,” I said, making my way down his steps.

“See you next week, Bill.”

I ended up cutting Mr. Hopkins’ grass every Wednesday morning that summer. My friends couldn’t believe it. I could hardly believe it myself. And what was even more incredible was that each time, when I was finished, Mr. Hopkins had lunch waiting for us on his front porch.

“I suspect I’m a bit of a mystery around here,” he said the first time we had lunch together.

"Yeah, you might say that."

"Well, I understand. What would you like to know about me, Bill?"

His question caught me by surprise.

"How long have you had that car?"

It was a stupid question but the first thing that popped into my head.

"I bought it new in 1938. Would you like to see it?"

"Yeah."

We walked the gravel path to a one-car garage behind his house. He struggled to lift the door. I helped him push it up.

And there it was, like some rare antiquity on display in a museum.

"It looks so old," I blurted out.

"It is. But it still runs well."

"Is that why you've kept it?"

"No."

"Why then?"

He told me he bought it when his son, his only child, was a boy and that he used to take his wife and son for long drives in the country on Sundays.

He told me that his son was killed during the war and that he lost his wife to cancer less than a year later. He had been living alone in that house ever since.

"I keep this car because it's my only link with the two people I've loved most in this world," he said. "You hold on to what means the most."

"I'm sorry for your loss."

"Thank you, Bill. Would you like to go for a ride?"

"Sure."

And that's the way it went every Wednesday that summer. I would cut Mr. Hopkins' grass, he would serve us lunch and we would go for a ride in his Roadmaster.

When my friends found out, they wanted a ride too. Who wouldn't? I asked Mr. Hopkins. He said yes.

And so every Wednesday afternoon, after Mr. Hopkins and I had had lunch, my friends would come down to his house and pile into the back seat, and Mr. Hopkins would take us all for a ride. I always got to sit in the front.

* * *

That winter, Mr. Hopkins passed away. In his will, he instructed that his assets be sold and the proceeds given to charity.

Except for one thing: his car. He gave that to me.

I keep it in my garage. It still runs well. Once a week, I take my kids and their friends for rides.

Communion

About a week before my father died, I went to see him in his apartment at the retirement community where he lived, as I did every day.

He lay, propped up, in a hospital bed. He was very weak, and his eyes were closed. My sister told him I was there. He started crying. He had always been stoic, but he got very emotional near the end.

“Good morning,” I said.

I kissed him on the head, held his hand and asked him if there was anything he needed.

“Yes,” he said softly. “Some Italian bread dipped in hot, black coffee."

This was a bit surprising because my father wasn't eating much at that point. But I wanted to honor his wish, so I went out to buy a loaf of Italian bread and a cup of Starbucks.

When I got back, he was ready to eat. However, he could no longer feed himself, so I broke the bread into small pieces, dipped them into the coffee and fed him. He really loved that bread.

My father ate Italian bread as a boy. His grandfather, an Italian immigrant, was a baker. I suspect he provided fresh bread for his whole family.

The experience of feeding my father that bread felt like communion — between my father, the dying man, and my father, the boy, and between the two of us. It felt sacred.

Spiritual, Not Religious

Pete Loman watched blue-gray plumes of incense smoke rise like swirling spirits over the casket of his late wife as the priest swung a metal censer suspended from three gold chains.

He remembered holding the censer open for his pastor when he was an altar boy so the priest could sprinkle powdery incense on charcoal discs which Pete had lit in the sacristy. It was a ritual Pete had nearly forgotten because he had not been to Mass or even inside a church for many years.

He had stopped going to church because of his wife, and now here she was, being blessed in the sanctuary of St. Augustine, a white pall draped over her casket, surrounded by dozens of family members and friends who had gathered to mourn her passing and pray for the repose of her soul.

Pete met Sarah Keller at a party at a mutual friend's house after work one Friday. Each caught the other's eye. They were both still dressed in business attire, he in a blue pinstriped suit befitting an investment banker, she in a black dress befitting a fashion designer. He had dark hair and an athletic build. She was blond and petite with a face as pretty as the models she dressed. His eyes were brown. Hers were blue. They both smiled easily.

They were happy to be seated across from one another for dinner. They discovered they had a lot in common. They were both from large families. They had both grown up in the Midwest and come to New York after taking master's degrees. They both lived alone in flats in Soho.

At first, Pete was struck by Sarah's beauty. Her skin glowed and her complexion was flawless, yet she wore little make-up. But the more they talked, the more he was drawn to her eyes. Not because they were lovely, although they were, but because of a certain sadness he detected there. It gave her depth and made Pete want to get to know her all the more.

As guests began to leave, Pete asked Sarah if he could call her sometime. She said yes, and they exchanged business cards. They shared an Uber back to Soho. She got dropped off first. As she got out, she reached over for his hand.

"I'll see you again," she said.

"Good night," Pete said, gently squeezing her small hand.

He woke up before dawn the next morning, thinking about her. He waited until 8:00, then sent her a text.

I know it's a long shot, but by any chance would you be free for dinner tonight?

They met that evening at an Italian restaurant in an industrial-chic building in Soho. Pete took an Uber, but it was close enough to Sarah's place that she could walk.

Over dinner, they talked about everything from their childhoods to their jobs. As they talked, they held each other's gaze. To Pete, it was as if everyone else in the restaurant didn't exist. It was a noisy place, but he was completely focused on her voice, soft as it was.

And then there were her eyes. The more he looked into them, the deeper they seemed to go. It was as if he could see into her soul. What's more, he felt as though she were inviting him in, to see something more than her outward beauty, to behold something mysterious. In her eyes, he again sensed a sadness, just as he had the evening before. It drew him in, not as someone to light the darkness, but as a companion to hold her hand.

The restaurant began to clear out.

"It's getting late," Pete said. "You must be tired."

"Do you have an early morning?" she asked.

"Not too early. I was thinking of going to 9:00 Mass at St. Patrick's."

"Are you religious?" she asked.

"Sort of."

"Sort of?"

"Well, I go to church once in a while, if that's what you mean."

"I'd call that religious."

"Well, I used to be a lot more religious."

"You're Catholic?"

"Yeah," he said. "I was raised Catholic."

"I was too, but I haven't been to Mass since my high school graduation."

"Do you still consider yourself a Catholic?"

"No," she said.

"Why?" he asked, hoping he was not intruding.

"Well, I used to say I'm spiritual, not religious. But lately, I'm not so sure I'm all that spiritual either."

"Do you believe in God?"

"I don't know," she said. "I'm just not sure anymore."

He felt their conversation was getting a little too personal and thought it might be best to change the subject.

"May I walk you home?" he asked.

"I'd like that," she said.

They left the restaurant and stepped out onto the sidewalk. It was a warm night. As they turned and started walking, their hands touched. Pete reached for her hand, and she slipped it into his. She smiled and held his hand tightly, leaning into him, as they strolled down the sidewalk together.

When they got to her apartment, he pulled out his cell phone and said, "I'll call an Uber."

She turned to him and looked up into his face, her big, blue eyes gleaming in the lamplight like two oceans lit up by the moon. She stood on her toes and kissed him gently and slowly on the cheek.

"Why don't you come in?" she whispered.

He slipped his phone into his pocket, cupped her face in his hands and kissed her on the lips.

"Okay," he said between kisses.

* * *

Soon, Pete and Sarah fell in love. Six months later, they moved into an apartment in the tony Park Slope neighborhood in Brooklyn. Six months later, Pete proposed. A year after that, they were married at the charming Picnic House in Prospect Park.

Pete had suggested they get married in church.

"No way," Sarah said.

"Why not?" Pete asked.

"I'm just not comfortable there," she said. "Besides, we'd have to go through Pre-Cana. The priest would grill me about why I haven't been to church in 10 years. That wouldn't end well."

Pete didn't argue. He hadn't been to church lately himself.

And so they got married in an old building in a park in a ceremony that was decidedly secular. Their parents weren't thrilled about that, but Pete and Sarah paid for everything, so their parents didn't really get a vote.

Pete and Sarah were very happy together. They both worked long hours, but they made a point of having dinner together every night they were both home, no matter how late it was. On weekends, they toured museums, took in concerts and plays and went shopping. Sometimes Pete joined Sarah at fashion shows, including in Milan and Paris. They loved to travel.

They spent a small fortune on furnishings for their apartment. Sarah worked with an interior decorator on a complete makeover, which took more than a year. She was ecstatic when *House Beautiful* decided to include their place in a splashy feature on urban living. She bought reprints and sent them to colleagues and clients.

Sarah and Pete loved showing off their place. They hosted dinner parties every few months. Unfortunately, their dining room was relatively small, so they could invite only two other couples at a time.

They solved this problem by buying a brownstone just a few blocks away in Brooklyn. They got a good deal at just under $2 million. Their friends and relatives thought it was a sure sign Pete and Sarah were ready to start a family, but they saw it strictly as a smart investment—and, of course, a way to host larger dinner parties.

Before they got married, Pete and Sarah had discussed the idea of having children. Sarah was always cool to it. But now that they were well established in their careers and in their mid-thirties, Pete thought he would bring up the idea again. He asked Sarah over breakfast one Sunday.

Without answering him directly, she said, "When was the last time you saw Ben and Emily?"

"I don't know," he said. "It's been a while."

"Yeah, like about two years. Do you know why?"

"No, why?"

"Because they have kids now," she said. "Nobody ever sees them anymore."

"I think it would be fun to have kids," he said. "And I think you'd be a great mother."

"Please," she said. "I'd be the worst mother of all time. I have no patience for kids, and I've grown accustomed to our lifestyle, Pete. I like it. I'm afraid of what raising a family would do to my career. Imagine if we had to get by on one salary. I mean you're making great money, but we'd have to give a lot of things up. We might even have to sell this place. And imagine what college tuition is going to cost in 20 years."

Sarah's neck was red. Pete knew that meant she was truly upset. He decided not to push the subject, at least not at the moment. *Maybe she'll change her mind,* he thought. *We've still got plenty of time.*

* * *

Just after her thirty-sixth birthday, Sarah had her annual check-up with her gynecologist, Dr. Anna Costello. Sarah told her she had been experiencing some tenderness and slight pain in her left breast. She hadn't had a mammogram, so Dr. Costello ordered one just to be safe.

The next day, Dr. Costello called Sarah at work.

"It's probably nothing to be worried about, but we're seeing some spots in both your breasts."

"Spots?" Sarah said, trying not to sound alarmed.

"Yes, small, white spots. It's possible they've been there a while and are no real consequence. Since you haven't had a mammogram before, we have nothing to compare this one to."

"So what should we do?"

"Well, I'd like to get a better look," Dr. Costello said. "So I think we should do an MRI."

"Okay. When?"

"I can schedule you for as soon as tomorrow."

"Okay. Let's do it tomorrow."

"Good. I'll have someone call you right back to confirm the time."

"Anna," Sarah said. "Do you think it's cancer?"

"I don't know. What I do know is that mammograms can sometimes give false positives for cancer, especially in younger patients, like you. So I don't think we should jump to any conclusions. I wish I could be more specific. We'll know a lot more after tomorrow."

* * *

The MRI showed stage 3 cancer in both breasts. Sarah and Pete met right away with an oncologist, Dr. Whitacre. His recommended treatment was chemotherapy, which Sarah received in a clinic over the course of 12 weeks. After that, she had another MRI to assess the results.

Unfortunately, the tumors were not "meaningfully changed," and Dr. Whitacre recommended a radical mastectomy, concluding more limited surgery would likely not be successful.

Six weeks after her surgery, Sarah saw Dr. Whitacre for a follow-up exam. Her blood results showed the presence of cancer. A full-body MRI showed tumors in her liver and lungs.

"What are our treatment options?" Pete asked, sitting next to Sarah.

"I think chemotherapy is our best course," Dr. Whitacre said. "It gives us the best way of killing cancer cells wherever they may be in Sarah's body."

"What are my chances of survival?" Sarah asked.

"If the chemotherapy is effective, 30%," he said.

"And if I don't do chemo again?" Sarah asked.

"You wouldn't make it, Sarah," he said.

"Let's do it then," she said, squeezing Pete's hand.

* * *

This time, Sarah's chemotherapy was administered in the hospital, four days at a time. There would be six treatments in all, with a week off in between. The whole thing would take three months.

Sarah had tolerated the first chemotherapy regimen fairly well and, for the most part, she was able to keep working. This new regimen, though, consisting of a new cocktail of toxic drugs, hit her very hard. She threw up every day, slept a lot and began losing weight rapidly. She had no choice but to stop working.

When Sarah was in the hospital, Pete visited her there every day. When he could, he worked from her hospital room. When he talked on the phone, he sometimes disturbed Sarah, so he began using any empty room he could find when he needed to make a call. It was hardly ideal, but he would rather be near her than not.

As the treatment wore on and Sarah grew weaker, Pete asked her if she would like to see a priest.

"No priest," she said.

He didn't bring it up again.

By the fifth week of treatment, Sarah was pale, weak and emaciated. One morning, Pete arrived with the breakfast she had ordered the night before: a fried egg on buttered wheat toast. Her sense of taste changed all the time, and she hated hospital food.

He was putting her food on a plate when she said, "Would you hold onto that, please? I think I need to sleep a little longer."

"Of course," he said, leaning down and kissing her bald head.

"Thank you," she said, drifting off to sleep.

Pete went down the hall and put Sarah's breakfast in a refrigerator in the nurses' lounge. He had grown used to storing food and drinks there.

When he got back to her room, Sarah was asleep. He looked down at her. She had a most peaceful look on her face. He sat down in a recliner and pulled out his laptop to get some work done.

A few minutes later, he heard Sarah say, "Wow."

He looked over at her. She was looking up at the ceiling.

"Are you okay?" Pete asked.

She lowered her gaze and turned her head toward him. He looked at her face. It was luminous. Then he looked into her eyes. They were bright and, for the first time in a very long time, there was no trace of sadness.

"Yeah," she said. "Was it real?"

"Was what real?"

"What I just saw," she said.

"I don't know. What did you see?"

"I saw God."

"God?"

"Yeah."

What did he look like?"

"It's hard to say. He isn't—he isn't any one thing."

Pete sat there, not sure what to say.

"He is everything," she said. "And everywhere."

She closed her eyes.

"I need to sleep some more," she said.

"Okay," he said. "I'll be right here."

She fell back to sleep, a most peaceful look once again on her face. This time, she slept for an hour.

Pete was just about to step out to make a call when he heard her say softly, "Good morning."

"Good morning," he said. "How are you feeling?"

"I feel nothing," she said.

"Let me call the nurse," he said.

"No, Pete," she said. "I'm okay. Just sit. I have something to tell you."

He got out of the recliner, pulled a wooden chair up to her bed and sat down beside her. He took her left hand in both of his hands.

"What is it?" he asked.

"I was wrong," she said. "There is a God, and I *am* spiritual."

Pete gently squeezed her hand.

"I'm still not religious," she said, with a little laugh. "But I am spiritual. We all are."

"We are? How do you know?"

"Because I've seen God. I saw him in the faces of children. He is here. He is alive in us."

"I believe you," Pete said, tears rolling down his cheeks.

"Pete, you have to do something for me," she said.

"What it is, Sarah?"

"You have to take everything I own and sell it and give the money to the poor."

"Everything?"

"Yes, everything."

"Why?"

"I told you once I didn't believe in God," she said. "But the truth is, I've made the things I own into a god, and I've been selfish. I want to give away everything I have. Will you do that for me?"

"Yes," he said. "I will."

"Thank you, Pete. You're a good man."

He gently squeezed her hand.

"I'm going back to sleep now," she said. "Good night."

"Good night, my love," he said, getting up, leaning over and kissing her on the cheek.

He went back to the recliner and sat down. He had never felt so tired. He lay back and fell into a deep sleep.

A little while later, he was awakened by a loud, shrill beep and the sound of an anxious voice.

"She's not breathing!" Sarah's nurse called into a speaker in the wall.

* * *

One evening, a few weeks after Sarah's funeral, Pete sat on the sofa in his living room, looking at a picture of the two of them, taken in Paris a few years earlier. They both looked so happy, and she looked so elegant. They had just finished watching a fashion show and, in her little black dress, Sarah looked like she could have been on the runway.

He was still grieving her loss, but knowing he had still not acted on her dying wish made his heart even heavier. But he wasn't sure how to go about giving away Sarah's wealth. After all, she had not been specific, and there was nothing in their will about it.

He thought back to his childhood, when he used to pray for enlightenment when he was uncertain about things. He used to pray in church. But then he went to Mass nearly every day. He hadn't been in a church since the funeral at St. Augustine's. It was the only time he'd been there. *Maybe I should go back.*

He went online to see when St. Augustine's offered Mass. During the week, there was a Mass every morning at 7:00. He decided he would go in the morning and ask God for guidance.

The church was just a few blocks away from his home, so Pete walked there the next morning. He got there about 6:45. There were two large, wooden doors at the entrance. An old man with long gray hair and a long beard in loose-fitting, tattered clothes was sitting on the doorstep, right between the two doors. There was a basket on the sidewalk in front of him.

Pete wasn't sure if he could step around the man in order to open one of the doors.

"Excuse me," he said.

"Going to church?" the beggar asked.

"Yes," Pete said.

"Doors don't open until just before seven."

Pete looked at his watch.

"You can wait here," said the beggar.

"I guess I will," Pete said.

He looked down into the basket. It was empty. He took out his wallet. The smallest bill he had was a five. He pulled it out and dropped it into the basket.

"Thank you," the beggar said.

"You're welcome."

A small boy, wearing a book bag on his back, was walking by them down the sidewalk.

"Good morning, King," the beggar said to him.

"Good morning, Mr. Ackmann," the boy said.

"Had breakfast?" the beggar asked.

"No," the boy replied.

"Got money for lunch?"

"No."

"Here," the beggar said, pulling the five out of his basket and handing it to the boy.

"Thank you!" said the boy.

"You're welcome, King. God be with you today."

Pete heard someone unlocking the doors from the inside.

"Are you coming in?" he asked the beggar.

"No," he said. "My church is out here."

Pete reached for the wrought iron door handle, then stopped. In his mind, he heard Sarah's voice.

I saw him in the faces of children.

He took out his wallet, pulled out all the money inside, and placed it in the beggar's basket.

"Thank you," said Mr. Ackmann. "That's going to make a lot of kids happy.

Theo

It is a confusing, anxious time. People distant from one another, wearing masks. People worried about their health and their livelihoods. People worried about the future.

You weren't due for another eight weeks. That was the plan anyway.

But you arrived when the time was right, and you were healthy and beautiful and perfect.

Your name is Theo, which means God. We were waiting for you, and you came when we needed you most.

You remind us God is with us. You remind us that, even in a chaotic and perilous time, life finds a way and joy abounds.

Fantasy

Everything is Real

David and Myrna Kaplan didn't survive the crash. But Sam, their eight-year-old daughter who was sitting in the back seat, did.

There were no seat belts in 1952, and she was thrown through the windshield. The collision broke bones throughout her body. Yet somehow she was alive when the ambulance arrived. The medics rushed her to Cook County Hospital, where a team of doctors immediately got to work.

They weren't concerned about her bones. Those could be repaired, and eventually they would heal. But one of her lungs was so badly damaged that they had to remove it, and her heart and other lung were in terrible shape.

"She won't make it through the night," said Dr. Charles Thomas, the chief of surgery.

Sam needed a miracle. More specifically, she needed a new heart and a new lung. An administrator had notified all the hospitals in the area of that need.

That night Chicago was being pummeled by a blizzard. It had caused the Kaplan's accident. Sadly, it was the kind of night when a healthy heart or lung might suddenly become available.

And yet, even then, it seemed Sam's fate was sealed. She had simply been born too soon. Medical journals would not record the first heart-lung transplant for another 29 years.

After eight hours of surgery, Sam's doctors concluded they had done all they could for her. A little after midnight, they turned her over to two operating room nurses, who now had the seemingly impossible task of keeping the little girl alive.

The nurses' names, embroidered on their scrubs, were Barbara Keith and Nell Lohman. Once the doctors left, they stepped over to Sam's bed to wheel her into recovery.

Nell released the brake, but Barbara grabbed the bed frame and held it in place.

"Wait," Barbara said.

Nell looked up at her. Barbara was looking at Sam's heavily bandaged face and holding her right hand. Nell looked down at Sam's face too. Then she reached out and took hold of her other hand. The two of them stood there, gently holding Sam's hands in silence.

Then the operating room door swung open, and in walked another doctor. He was in scrubs. His mouth and nose were covered. His eyes had the intense look of a man on a mission. "Dr. Joshua Simon" was embroidered on his chest pocket. Neither Barbara nor Nell had met Dr. Simon, but they certainly knew his name. He was one of the finest surgeons in the country. He worked at Michael Reese, a research and teaching hospital just a few miles away.

"Good morning, doctor," said Barbara. "Are you here for Sam?"

He nodded. Then a second doctor came through the doors, wheeling in a strange-looking machine, a metal cart with black dials and plastic tubes extending from the top like tentacles. A third doctor followed close behind. He was carrying a metal cooler.

Dr. Simon turned toward the nurses.

"Nurse Keith, Nurse Lohman. I know it's late. Would you please assist me in this procedure?"

"Of course, doctor."

"Of course."

They wheeled Sam back into the operating room, lifted her back onto the table and prepared her for surgery. Dr. Simon administered the anesthesia.

A few minutes later, he re-opened the incision in Sam's chest and spread her ribs, giving him access to her heart and lung. The second doctor then connected her to the machine. Dr. Simon carefully removed Sam's failing organs.

The nurses felt dizzy, not from the blood but from witnessing a procedure they had never seen and would have thought was impossible.

Then the third doctor handed Dr. Simon the donor heart and lung and helped him sew them into place. A few minutes later, the new organs began to warm up, and the lung began to inflate. The heart began to beat rapidly and irregularly. Dr. Simon asked for a paddle. He used it to apply a small electric shock to Sam's heart, which then began beating properly.

With the new organs functioning normally, the second doctor removed the machine. Dr. Simon closed Sam's chest.

"Take good care of this little girl," he said.

Then as quickly as they had come in, Dr. Simon and his associates left.

* * *

"How is the patient?" Dr. Thomas asked as he entered the intensive care unit during his morning rounds.

"She's stable," said the attending nurse.

"What?"

"Yes, haven't you heard? Dr. Simon performed a heart-lung transplant on her last night. It's a miracle."

"A what?"

"A heart-lung transplant."

"Dr. Simon?"

"Yes, from Michael Reese."

Dr. Thomas left the room and hurried over to the nurses station.

"Nurse, get Dr. Simon at Michael Reese on the phone for me."

"Yes, doctor."

She picked up the phone and dialed.

"This is Marilyn Pemberton calling for Dr. Thomas from Cook County Hospital. May I speak with Dr. Simon, please?"

She looked up at Dr. Thomas. There was a voice at the other end of the line.

"Excuse me?" the nurse said with a look of disbelief. "Are you sure?"

"What is it?" Dr. Thomas asked.

She turned away.

"Very well," she said softly. "I'm sorry. Thank you."

She hung up the phone.

"What did they say?" Dr. Thomas asked.

She looked up.

"They said Dr. Simon and his son were killed in a car accident in the blizzard yesterday afternoon."

* * *

"Everything you can imagine is real," Picasso said.

People and places, ideas and events, hopes and fears. An extraordinary surgeon who performed one final operation to save a little girl who had been given up for dead by using a machine which had not yet been invented, even as his own obituary was being written.

All we can imagine is real.

Everything is real.

Masks

At first, no one wanted to wear one. Masks were a nuisance. They were ugly, and you couldn't make out people's facial expressions. It was like living in a world of strangers.

But as the pandemic dragged on, people got used to them. They even began to seek out masks with certain colors, shapes and designs. Masks became fashionable. They made personal statements.

People grew attached to their masks. They were no longer an accessory. They had become part of people's identity.

When the pandemic finally passed, few took off their masks for fear of not recognizing anyone, including themselves.

Tranquility Room

Bill Armstrong looked down at his ringing cell phone. *Spam.* He got up and turned off the TV, then sat back down and opened his laptop. The email icon at the bottom of the screen showed 43 new messages.

"Damn!" he said.

"Sorry, I'm having trouble understanding you right now," Alexa said. "Please try a little later."

Bill grumbled, hoping Alexa wouldn't hear, and logged on for his next Zoom meeting. He could hear his wife on a Zoom call in the next room and his kids in school online in their bedrooms.

The doorbell rang. Charley barked madly at the front door. Bill looked out the window and saw an Amazon truck pulling away.

This is my life, he thought. There's got to be a better way.

* * *

"I feel like I'm being bombarded," Bill told his wife Janice that evening after the kids were in bed.

"By what?" she said.

"Bad news. Non-stop emails and texts. Social media. I think all the noise is making me crazy."

"Why don't you unplug?"

"I've tried that," he said. "Easier said than done. The world isn't going to stop just because I turn off the TV."

"Well, you're right. But you've got to find a way to give yourself some peace."

"I know."

She came over, sat down beside him on the sofa and put her arms around him.

"I worry about you, Bill. You seem down lately."

"I feel worn down," he said. "I feel worn down by all the noise. I need a break."

"Maybe we should go away for a long weekend," she said.

He thought about it for a moment. But he knew with the pandemic raging, their options were limited. Besides, no matter where they went, the bad news on TV, the vitriol of social media and the incessant barrage of texts and emails would follow them.

"Maybe," he said. "We'll figure something out."

"I love you," she said, kissing him on the cheek.

"I love you too," he said, his phone dinging with the receipt of another text message.

* * *

One morning, when the kids and Janice were online, Bill went down to his basement simply to get away from the busyness and noise in his house.

The only time he went into his basement was to watch TV, usually a big game. He hadn't been down there in a while.

Now he walked past his widescreen TV and came to the door to a small room Janice used for crafts. He hadn't been in it in years.

He opened the door and flipped on the light. The room was cluttered with colored paper, paints, brushes, markers, glue sticks, scissors, paper cups, pipe cleaners, popsicle sticks, cardboard boxes and plastic bins. The only furniture was a small table, a lamp and a wooden chair with a loose seat cushion.

The room had one small window. Sunlight streamed in. As Bill looked around, he was struck by the stillness.

He stepped over to the table, pulled out the chair and sat down. Aside from occasional soft footsteps upstairs, there was no sound at all.

Something outside, through the window, caught his eye. It was a large maple tree in his backyard whose bare branches were swaying in the wind. He hadn't paid much attention to that tree before. Now it looked as if it were beckoning him.

Bill got up, turned off the lamp and sat back down. He thought of a class Janice had taken in meditation when they were first married. She had talked him into going once. Bill had found the experience awkward.

He had tried hard to clear his mind, even though the instructor had said, "When your mind wanders, simply return your attention to your breath as an anchor to the present."

Bill had been unable to do that. Now, desperate for some peace in his life, he decided to try again.

He closed his eyes, put his feet flat on the floor and sat up straight. He rested his palms on his thighs. He took a deep breath.

He thought about the Zoom call he would have in an hour.

But he remembered what the instructor had said and brought his mind back to his breathing.

He thought about the spike in new Covid cases being reported that morning.

Again, he brought his mind back to his breathing.

He thought about the latest violence in Portland.

Then, once again, he brought his mind back to his breathing.

His mind kept wandering, but he kept returning his attention to his breath.

After about 15 minutes of this, Bill opened his eyes and went upstairs.

* * *

"Sure," Janice said later that morning. "I don't use it much anymore. Just keep all my stuff together in the storage room."

That afternoon Bill went back downstairs and cleared out Janice's crafts room, leaving only the table and chair. He even took out the lamp because the sunlight through the window was sufficient.

The following morning, Bill went down to the room he'd cleared out and tried again to meditate. His mind kept wandering. But each time it did, Bill returned to his breath.

He did this morning after morning. Over a period of months, he began to learn not to try to clear his mind but to train it to notice when he was lost in thought and then shift his awareness to the present.

He was able to do this in a room free of electronic devices, away from social media and all the trappings of his everyday life. Bill called it his tranquility room.

Of course, every time he went back upstairs, the noise was still there. Covid was still killing people, the "talking heads" on TV were still screaming and the news was still bad.

But Bill began to accept the fact that this noise would always be there. He knew he couldn't stop it. But he realized he could stop listening to it, if only for a short time.

Day by day, Bill began to recover a sense of peace he thought was no longer possible. He began to let go of the things that had been bombarding him. And his heart began to feel open again.

As the pandemic subsided and people got back together, Bill was different, and the world seemed different too.

Life seemed a little slower. Bill listened more closely to his friends and loved ones, and he shared himself more openly. He was more present in whatever he was doing.

That year, through the window in his tranquility room, Bill watched the maple tree in his backyard bud, bloom and leaf out. Then he watched its leaves change colors and let go. He had nearly forgotten life could be like this.

Crazy

After my accident in 1972, I fell into a coma. A few days ago, I woke up.

How I've managed to stay alive, I don't know. For nearly 50 years, as I lay in bed, I wasn't able to see or speak or move. But I heard everything, and I followed what was happening in the world.

When I awoke, I asked my nurse why she wasn't wearing a mask.

"A mask?" she said.

"For Covid."

"For what?"

I tried to explain, but she seemed oblivious. Maybe it was the shock of me waking up.

Over the next two days, I talked to a slew of doctors. They quizzed me about what I claimed I'd heard while I was unconscious.

I told them everything. I told them about Watergate and three presidential impeachments, the Internet and cell phones, 9/11 and Covid-19.

They seemed not to know about any of these things. In fact, they seemed skeptical of everything I said.

I wished someone would come to my aid. I wished my parents were around. It still made me sad that I'd missed their funerals. It made me sad that my friends stopped coming by to see me decades ago. I've been alone a very long time.

I heard voices in the hallway outside my door. I heard my name. Finally, a doctor came in and told me they'd decided to transfer me to a special facility for "observation and treatment."

My new room is nearly bare. There's a calendar on my wall. I stare at it a lot. It's for the year 1972. It looks new.

Walk in the Grass

George and Jane met in a park, walking across the grass on a sunny day.

Now, five years later, it was time to start a family. For most young couples, this would be such a happy moment. But most young couples aren't on a spaceship, just beginning a 30-year odyssey to Pluto and back.

They had signed up for this adventure knowing their children and grandchildren would be born in space. They would all be pioneers. The idea seemed so bold and exciting.

But now, watching the Earth shrink in the distance, George and Jane wanted only to feel the soft grass beneath their feet.

Well-Being

I woke up. I couldn't speak or see. But I could hear a woman's voice.

"Mr. Douglas, can you hear me?"

"Yes," I mumbled, barely able to move my lips.

I heard someone gasp.

"Mr. Douglas, can you open your eyes?"

My eyelids felt like sand bags. But I wanted to see. Raising my eyebrows, with all the strength I had in the muscles of my forehead, I slowly opened my eyes.

In the dim light, I could see two women dressed in white looking down at me. I was lying in bed, and they were standing at my sides.

"Mr. Douglas," said the one on the left. "Can you hear me?"

"Yes," I said, more clearly this time. "And I can see you too."

The two women looked at each other, as if they were not sure what to say.

"Where am I?" I said.

"You're in a room in a 500 ward in sector four," said the woman on my right.

"Brenda!" said the other woman, sounding irritated. "He's not going to know what that means. Let me handle this."

I looked up at the woman on my left.

"Mr. Douglas, my name is Cathy. Brenda and I are your nurses here. You've been asleep, in a coma actually, for a very long time."

"How long?"

"Five hundred years," Cathy said.

"Five hundred years!" I cried. "That's impossible! Where am I? Where is my wife? Where are my children?"

"Mr. Douglas," Cathy said. "Let me explain. Five hundred years ago, you were in a car accident. The surgeons were able to save your life, but you slipped into a coma and never regained consciousness. Until now."

I blinked and looked around. My head and back were slightly raised. A plastic tube was taped to my right arm, which looked so scrawny. Another tube protruded from under the thin blanket which covered me. Both tubes were connected to a device at the foot of my bed. I could see nothing else in the room except two straight-backed chairs.

"Where am I?" I said. "What is this place?"

Brenda looked at Cathy, who nodded.

"Mr. Douglas," said Brenda. "The world is very different from the one you've known. It's going to take time for you to fully understand the changes. But let me start with the basics."

"Okay."

"First, you no longer live in the United States because that country, like every country from your time, no longer exists. The world is now divided into sectors. We are in sector four."

"Sectors?"

"Yes. They were designated about 300 years ago. There are 12 sectors in all."

"Why sectors?"

"They were decreed by the tribunal after the great redistribution."

"The what?"

"Mr. Douglas," said Cathy, waving Brenda off. "Let's step back for a moment. When you had your accident, there were nearly seven and a half billion people in the world. Half of the world's wealth was owned by one percent of those people. About 30 percent of people in the world were overweight or obese. About 13 percent were starving. About half the world had no access to health care. Our planet was warming at an alarming rate. And we were on the brink of blowing ourselves up with nuclear weapons."

"The world was a mess," Brenda chimed in.

Cathy looked annoyed.

"People had had enough," Cathy said. "They realized we were on a path to self-destruction. So they began to demand major reforms. But governments weren't willing to make the kinds of reforms people were after, so the people banded together and took control. They dissolved their national constitutions and set up a tribunal to oversee a new world order. Are you with me so far, Mr. Douglas?"

"I'm not sure," I said. "Can you give me a few examples of how the world is now?"

"Certainly," said Cathy.

She looked at Brenda and nodded.

"Mr. Douglas," said Brenda, "let me start by telling you that our mantra is well-being. Well-being for everyone and everything on our planet."

"Well-being?"

"Yes. It has fallen to all of us to take care of every man, woman and child on earth as well as the earth itself."

"How do we do that?" I said.

"It's simple really," Brenda said. "For example, every person is given enough food to ensure an adequate number of calories a day and in the right nutritional balance."

"That alone is a big change," Cathy chimed in.

Now Brenda looked at Cathy.

"Sorry," Cathy said. "Go ahead."

"Income is capped so that a living wage is enjoyed by all. All income is taxed at 15 percent. All tax revenue is shared to pay for ways to enhance the well-being of people everywhere."

"Such as?" I said.

"Food, shelter, security, education, health care and renewable energy," Brenda said. "These are our common priorities."

"But if people can make only a living wage, is there enough money to go around?"

"Plenty. Partly because people need far less these days. And partly because there are fewer people."

"Fewer?"

"Far fewer," Brenda said. "The world's population is back down to about five billion."

"It's an optimal number," Cathy said.

I didn't have the strength to ask how the world's population was cut so dramatically or kept in check. So I simply said, "How is it working?"

"Very well," Cathy said. "You yourself are a living example of the benefits of the advances we've made in health care."

"How so?"

"When you had your accident," said Cathy, "the average lifespan of a man in the United States was about 78 years. Now, we're not even sure what the upward limit is."

"What do you mean?"

"Well," said Brenda, "for example, you are now 542 years old, Mr. Douglas. And I must say you are still in remarkably good health."

"You mean there are others as old as me?"

"Not many," Cathy said. "You're one of the oldest people on Earth. But given the pace of the advancement of our genomic and health care technologies, there is no reason to set an upward limit on life expectancy."

I blinked.

"Where am I? I mean what kind of a place is this?"

"You are in a special facility dedicated to the care of people who have reached their five-hundredth year," Brenda said.

"In sector four," Cathy added.

"What do people like me do here?"

The two nurses looked at each other.

"Nothing really," Cathy said.

"Nothing?"

"That's right," Brenda said. "You worked hard as a young man, Mr. Douglas. You provided for your family, and you paid taxes. If would be unfair for us not to take care of you now, just as we would take care of anyone."

"Anyone?" I said.

"Yes, anyone," Cathy said. "That's the idea. Equality in every way."

"Total equality," Brenda added.

I was having a hard time understanding.

"Where is my wife? Where are my children?"

The nurses looked at each other.

"Your wife and children are gone, Mr. Douglas," Cathy said. "I am sorry."

"Gone? When?"

"They died more than 400 years ago," Brenda said. "Unlike you, they were not able to benefit from the medical advances we've made over the past 500 years. Unfortunately, they died too soon. They were among the last of the pre-tribunal era people, before we could get everything organized and everyone in the system."

"I am sorry, Mr. Douglas," Cathy said.

It seemed I had just kissed my wife and children goodbye that morning. My eyes welled with tears.

"Then why am I still alive?"

"You survived in a coma just long enough to begin to receive DNA infusions," Cathy said. "DNA from your younger self, Mr. Douglas. These days, when a baby is born, DNA is taken and injected back into his or her body over the course of centuries. We were able to take samples of your DNA when you were in your sixties. That is the DNA we continue to inject periodically and why you'll continue to be in your sixties, possibly forever."

"Forever?"

"Well, yes, theoretically," Brenda said.

"But I don't want to live like this forever!"

The nurses looked at each other quizzically.

"Mr. Douglas," Cathy said. "You are in relatively good health. We give you proper nutrition every day. You want for nothing because, in accordance with the rules, others pay for everything you need. The Earth is cooling. Our air and water are clean, and the world is at peace. What more could you ask for?"

I looked back at forth at the nurses. I looked more closely at their faces. They were flawless. I could not tell their age.

"But I'm not *supposed* to live here forever! My wife and children are gone. I should be gone too. I should be with them."

"But Mr. Douglas," Cathy said. "You are not with them. You are here, with us."

"And it is our duty, Mr. Douglas," Brenda said, adjusting a dial on the device at the foot of my bed, "to ensure your well-being."

Rest Stop Ghosts

I pulled into the parking space at the rest stop but couldn't open my door. The front door of a van parked next to me was wide open, inches from my door. A woman was standing on the running board, facing the back of the van, keeping close watch as her kids got out.

"Don't touch anything!" she yelled, as they ran toward the restrooms.

"Hurry up!" shouted a man standing on the other side of the van.

The scene reminded me of our family vacations when I was kid. We traveled by station wagon. My dad was always hellbent on getting to our destination. He would drive long stretches between stops, and we often took breaks at rest areas. Dad was always on us to hurry up, and Mom was always telling us not to touch anything.

Stepping down from the running board, the woman next to me finally realized her door was blocking me.

"Oh, I'm sorry," she said, closing it.

I smiled and opened my door.

"It's okay. I'm not in a hurry."

These rest areas used to creep me out. *How silly*, I thought.

Not that we spent much time there. We'd pull in, and Dad and one of my older brothers would grab a cooler out of the back of the wagon and lug it to a picnic table. By the time they got there, Mom had already covered the top with a plastic tablecloth and was unpacking our picnic basket.

She made us go to the bathroom and wash up both before and after lunch.

"Don't touch anything!" she would call after us.

"And hurry up!" Dad would add.

We hated going into those bathrooms. There was always a creepy-looking guy in there mopping the floor. No matter the location of the rest stop, he always seemed to look the same too, with a mustache and a baggy gray uniform.

"Watch your step," he would say in a gravelly voice.

Then there were the vending machines. They were usually lined up in a little cinderblock building with glass walls. My parents never let us buy anything.

We never lingered at those rest stops. Mom and Dad were always eager to get back on the road, and we were okay with that. There were always strange-looking people lurking about. We never strayed far from my parents.

Now I grinned remembering it. *How childish to be so afraid.* As I stood at the urinal, I heard water dripping behind me. I looked around and saw a guy in a gray uniform pressing down on the handle on the top of a bucket, wringing water out of a mop.

Funny, I hadn't seen him when I came in.

"Watch your step," he said in a coarse voice, flopping the mop down on the floor.

He had a mustache.

I zipped up, ran water over my hands and got out of there. I avoided touching anything.

I still had a few hours of driving ahead of me, and I was tired, so I decided to grab a cup of coffee. The vending machines were in a small, cinderblock building. I stepped inside. I pulled a dollar bill out of my wallet, inserted it in the coffee machine and pressed the button.

As I waited for the coffee to dispense, I heard the door open. An obese, bearded man stepped in. He was wearing a jeans jacket and a ball cap. Grunting, he waddled back and forth behind me. Then he stepped up to one of the candy machines and shoved his chubby finger into the metal slot for change. I grabbed my coffee and left.

Outside, people were shuffling along the sidewalks to and from the restrooms. Some were meandering in the grass. No one was saying a word. Everyone was moving slowly, like zombies.

A skeleton-thin man sat on the top of a picnic table, smoking a cigarette. A crow cawed. A big dog, which looked like a wolf, started barking. The sky grew overcast. Thunder rolled in the distance. Out of nowhere, the wind kicked up, shaking tree limbs and rustling leaves.

I hurried back to my car, ducked inside and locked it. As I backed out, I could see the faces of dozens of people, all of them slightly swaying and looking my way. My headlights illuminated their eyes, which glowed like iridescent rosary beads.

I noticed the van was gone. In its place was an old Pontiac station wagon.

The Pin Insulator

As soon as his aunt lay down for her afternoon nap, John took off on his bike. He sliced through his subdivision, then made his way through the narrower streets of the older neighborhoods, where his mother had grown up. Her father had grown up on one of the farms just beyond.

He had heard there is a river beyond the farmland. He had always wanted to see it. But his mother would never let him go that far, not even with friends. Now, though, his parents were gone. They were attending his grandfather's funeral, and his aunt, who was in charge for a few days, liked to take very long naps.

John came to a cornfield at the edge of the older neighborhood. He laid his bike down and walked between the rows of corn toward where he had heard the river would be.

At the other end of the cornfield lay a meadow filled with tall grasses, milkweed and wildflowers. In the distance, he could see a thicket of oak trees. Off to the right stood a red barn and a white farmhouse.

Something shiny caught his eye. Curious, he made his way through the tall grass to check out whatever was glistening in the afternoon sun.

Whatever it was, it was attached to the top of a fallen telephone pole whose end was jutting up through the grass. As he got closer, he realized the pole was resting on another one on the ground. There was a whole line of fallen telephone poles that stretched across the meadow, obscured by the grass.

Now he could see what was glistening. It was a fist-sized, aqua-colored, cylindrical glass object, rounded at the end. It was sitting on a wooden pin which extended from the cross arm of the telephone pole. Looking more closely, John could see that the inside of the glass was threaded, and he decided to try to unscrew it.

But as soon as he touched it, a current shot though his body and knocked him backwards. For a few moments, he could see nothing but a white light. Then everything around him came back into focus.

Except that now the telephone poles were all standing, with wires stretching between them. Glass objects, just like the one he had seen, dotted the cross arms of every pole.

John thought he was seeing things. Then he heard the splash of water. It was coming from beyond the trees up ahead. It must be the river, he thought.

As he headed toward the trees, he heard someone singing. It sounded like the voice of a boy.

He walked through the trees, and there was the river. Not far from the bank stood a boy in water up to his waist.

"Hey!" the boy yelled, spotting John.

"Hey!"

"Want to go swimming? The water's warm today."

"I didn't bring my trunks."

"Trunks? Who needs trunks? I swim naked. Actually, I can't swim. But I don't go out very far. Do you know how to swim?"

"Yeah."

"Then lose your clothes and take a dip. It feels great!"

Being a boy whose parents were out of town, John took off his clothes and waded in.

"What's your name?" he said to the boy in the water.

"Henry. What's yours?"

"John."

"Watch yourself, John. The rocks are slippery, and the bottom drops off in a hurry."

"Do you live around here?" John said.

"Yeah. My family lives on the farm just beyond those trees."

"Can I ask you something about those telephone poles over there?"

"Shoot."

"Have they always been standing up like that?"

"What do you mean?"

"Just a little while ago, I could have sworn they were all down on the ground."

"What are you talking about? That's how we get our electricity out here."

Just then Henry disappeared under the water. When he bobbed back up, his arms flailing, he cried, "Help!"

From the panicked look on his face, John knew he wasn't joking. He'd slipped into a deep pool in the river.

"Hang on!" he cried, diving in.

John was a strong swimmer. He grabbed Henry around the chest and side stroked towards shore. Soon, they were back in shallow water, standing up.

"That was close," John said.

"Too close," Henry coughed. "Thanks for saving me."

"No problem."

Henry lay down on the grassy bank, still catching his breath.

"Now what were you saying about those telephone poles?"

"Oh, nothing. I took a fall back there. I think I might have been seeing things."

"Well, those poles better be standing. We depend on them for our electric and telephone. Plus, I like climbing them. Well, I've got to get home," he said, pulling on his undershirt. It was the old sleeveless, tank top kind.

"Me too," John said, stepping into his jeans. "It was good to meet you, Henry. I'm glad you're okay."

"Good to meet you too, John. Thanks for being here today."

John's parents got home the next morning. They brought back some of his grandfather's things, including a bunch of old photographs. His mother spread them out on the dining room table.

John was astonished to see a glass object just like the one he had seen yesterday.

"What's that?" he asked.

"That's a pin insulator."

"A what?"

"A pin insulator. They used to use them on telephone poles to keep the wires in place."

"Where'd you get it?"

"It was grandpa's. He loved telling us how he used to climb up telephone poles as a boy and crawl out on the crossbeam to get these things. He used this one as a paperweight for years. I remember it from when I was growing up. I thought you might like to have it."

John went over to the table and picked it up. It was heavy and felt thick in his hands. Then he looked down at the photographs.

"Who's this?" he asked.

"That's grandpa, probably when he was about your age."

John gasped. It was Henry.

Carey

"Morning, Carey," I said.

"Good morning, Raymond," she said. "How are you?"

"Fine. And you?"

"I am fine. Thank you. Are you ready for breakfast?"

"Yes."

"Good. I made your favorite."

"Scrambled eggs and toast?"

"Lightly buttered."

"Orange juice?"

"No pulp."

"Thank you, Carey," I said as she carefully placed the tray on the one over my bed.

"Will there be anything else, Raymond?"

"Not right now."

My friends are all gone. No one ever visits anymore. What would I do without Carey?

"I will return soon, Raymond," she said, making a graceful exit.

So sweet. So thoughtful. So lifelike.

The Moon and the Birds

Helen fluffed the pillow behind her, sat upright in bed and wondered what day it was.

She knew she should have sold the farm years ago and that by now she should be living in a retirement center or someplace where people could take care of her. But she kept putting it off, and there was no one around to help make it happen. Someone from church still brought food once a week. But lately she was having a hard time fixing it, and she didn't have much of an appetite anyway. Some days, she simply stayed in bed. She was too weak to get out.

For a moment, she thought about watching TV. But she found the news too depressing. She considered reading, but lately she was having a hard time seeing the words, and her hands were too shaky to hold a book.

She looked over at the framed pictures on her nightstand, photos of her husband, Charlie, and her children, Michael and Susan. How she wished they were there with her now.

How she wished Charlie were there to kiss her good morning, as he always did before leaving to work in the fields or tend the animals. Oh, to feel his lips on her cheek or hear him whisper "I love you."

It had been more than 10 years. And she hadn't had the strength to visit his grave near the woods for nearly three weeks now. She missed him so.

Thinking of Charlie always made her think of the moon. When they were young, he had courted her under the moon. They danced by its light. He proposed to her under a full moon. When their kids were little, after they'd put them to bed, Charlie and Helen would sit together on the swing on the back porch and look up at the moon. And when their kids left home, they would cuddle in that same swing, like young lovers, gently rocking under the moonlight.

"Gaze at it, Helen," he would say. "Let it draw you in. The moon is eternal. If you let yourself be drawn in, you too will live forever."

She would smile at him when he would talk that way. But he didn't mind. He was sure he was right. He claimed he could feel the moon's gravitational pull. He claimed he could feel the moon drawing him toward heaven.

If Charlie had a thing for the moon, Michael and Susan had a thing for birds. Helen didn't know where Charlie got his ideas about the moon. But she felt responsible for the way her children felt about birds.

When they were little, she would take them into the fields. There they would spot cardinals, orioles, whippoorwills, yellow-headed blackbirds, barn swallows, robins, gold finches, wrens, blue jays, sparrows, hawks and black-capped chickadees. Whenever her children saw a bird, they would stop and study it and listen intently. They were captivated by birds. They learned all their names and spent hours learning to mimic their songs.

They got so good at it that sometimes Helen would look out their kitchen window, hearing some bird, only to find Michael or Susan, crouching in the bushes, whistling, tweeting or chirping. Of course, they were watching for her the whole time, and they would laugh when she spotted them hiding, delighted that they had fooled her. It was a game they played all the while they were growing up.

Her memories of that time were so real that sometimes when Helen would hear birds singing through her open bedroom window, she would think Michael and Susan had come home to visit. And sometimes when she would see the moon through the curtains, she would think Charlie was sitting next to her on the porch swing.

Tonight she felt so tired. She hadn't done a thing all day, not even left her bed. She had simply sat there, thinking about her husband and her children, missing them, loving them, longing to be with them again.

Through her open window, she heard two birds singing together. A sparrow and a wren, she thought. Funny, she had never heard them singing together before, least of all at night.

Then she looked up and saw a harvest moon, so large in the sky that she felt she could reach out and touch it.

Helen smiled and closed her eyes. She saw the faces of her husband and children. They looked so happy to see her.

Charlie extended his hand and, without words, asked her to dance. Michael and Susan were running towards her, though the moonlit fields, laughing and calling her name. Birds, all the birds of their childhood, glided around them, guiding their way.

Helen took Charlie's hand, and they danced in the moonlight. Then she knelt down and gathered her children in, as birds filled the air with a song of sweet communion.

Journey

Flashpoint

Pete and I had been kayaking for about an hour in Glacier Bay, Alaska, when we spotted something in the distance. It looked like a shadow on the water. At first, I thought it was a boat. But then it disappeared, then reappeared. It was probably 200 yards away. Whatever it was, it was big.

"Holy crap!" Pete cried. "I think it's a whale!"

I felt my chest tighten. I felt dizzy. I had just learned to control my lifelong fear of water, and now it came rushing back. I had an overwhelming urge to get the hell out of this little boat and feel the Earth beneath my feet.

I looked around to find our group. Once again, Pete and I had wandered off. We were 100 yards from the others. And we were all a mile from the small ship that all 14 of us called home that week.

"Pete, let's get back with the group."

"No way," he said. "We're staying put. John said if we see a whale, we shouldn't move."

"Maybe it's not a whale."

"You're right. It's not a whale. It's three whales!"

Sure enough, I now saw three whales in the distance, and they were heading our way.

Damn! Sometimes I hated it when Pete was right.

* * *

A week before, Pete and I had put our laptops away, kissed our families goodbye and set out for Alaska. It was July 2007.

I had known Pete for nearly 20 years. For much of that time, he had been asking me to take this trip with him. Pete had been to Alaska twice. He raved about it. His voice would get high-pitched, like a kid, when he told me about glaciers "calving icebergs," huge chunks of ice breaking off the end of glaciers and plummeting into the bay.

"They're as big as a school bus!" he would exclaim, stretching his arms and thrusting his fingers into the air. "You're kayaking along and, all of a sudden, crack! The next thing you know, that ice hits the water, and the impact creates a huge wave. If you're too close, it'll swamp you and flip your boat. But if you're just far enough away, you can ride it. What a rush!"

Breathlessly, Pete told me about the time he dove off the side of a boat without a wetsuit into the frigid water below.

"It was a sunny day, but the water was 38 degrees," he said. "There was ice floating in it. Without a wetsuit, you've only got a few minutes to live. After a minute, your arms begin to freeze. So you can't jump out too far, and you have to swim fast."

Pete said when he hit the water, it was like being in another world.

"Everything is deep blue. You can't believe how cold that water is. At first, it stings like hell. Then you can't feel a thing. And you can't hear anything, except for the beating of your heart. Boomp, boomp. Boomp, boomp. Boomp, boomp," Pete murmured, thumping his chest.

Yet Pete kept diving. He forced himself to go deeper until he could go no farther. When he finally surfaced, he heard the cheers of the other passengers watching from the safety of the deck.

"I was out farther than I thought," he said.

When he realized just how far from the boat he was, Pete tried to swim hard. He was a strong swimmer. But now his arms felt like lead, and he struggled to lift them. Tiny icebergs bounced off his 250-pound body. He felt like he was in slow motion. By the time he got close to the boat, he could barely move, and he could no longer feel his arms.

"But our guide was watching everything," he said, smiling, "and he pulled me up on deck just in time. It was incredible!"

Of course, none of us believed him. Who would do something so crazy?

But Pete had proof: a photograph someone on the boat had taken of him in the water. He carried it, folded and tattered, in his wallet. Sure enough, there was Pete — a walrus of a man, mustache and all, his blanched, bare torso jutting out of the icy water, his right arm extended forward and up, his hand grasping another man's hand, his lips blue, his thinning hair glazed on his forehead, his eyes half-closed. He was probably seconds from hypothermia. But on his face was a big grin that said: I made it — and I can't wait to tell you about it.

For years, Pete had tried to persuade me to go with him to Alaska. I was tempted. It certainly looked stunning in his pictures. But his stories — about glaciers calving, water so cold it could kill you, being chased in his kayak by a sea lion, hikers falling into deep crevasses — also scared the hell out of me.

Pete was a risk taker. In the 1980s, he had founded an advertising agency in Cincinnati, our hometown. Early on, he nearly lost everything. Once he had to mortgage his house to pay his employees. He always put others first. I admired that.

But Pete stuck with it, and it worked. He built his company into Cincinnati's largest ad agency. It became *the* place to work, especially if you were young in the business. It wasn't just successful. It was hip. Employees brainstormed while shooting pool in a conference room, Pete right along with them. He might have been old enough to be their father. But the other dads didn't sport a goatee, dress in black, tweet and bring home a Gold Lion from Cannes.

Pete's years of hard work paid off. In 2005, he sold his company to the biggest ad agency in the world for a small fortune. Pete's risk was also his reward.

I, on the other hand, was not a risk taker. I worked in public relations for one of the most conservative companies in the world. In 2007, I had been there for 27 years.

And while Pete was diving into ice water and being chased by sea lions, I was busy defending the safety of the latest controversial ingredient in shampoo.

But as different as our lives were, as different as we were, Pete and I became the best of friends. Part of it, I think, is that we balanced each other out.

But there was something more. I think Pete and I also became good friends because we could just be ourselves with each other.

At work, and even at home, we had roles to play, important roles, roles we loved. But the more we got into these roles, the harder it was to get out of them, to find an escape hatch, a way to step out and let down, to talk freely, to share problems without feeling obliged to also propose solutions.

This was the safe haven that Pete and I found, a place where we could be unguarded and unvarnished, a place void of pretense, a place of vulnerability, a place of pure acceptance.

We met through our wives, who met through our children. But I don't remember ever meeting Pete. Suddenly, he was just there, and we were hanging out, running together, drinking wine and telling jokes. We went to movies, dinner and ballgames together. We played golf, badly, together. We argued a lot, especially over politics and religion. We talked or texted nearly every day. And at some point, we became best friends.

Pete kept asking me to go to Alaska, and I kept saying no. We would have to go in July, he said, the only time it was warm enough. Every July, I'd have a good excuse.

But the truth is: I was wary. For starters, I'm a poor swimmer, and I'm uncomfortable in the water. I wasn't sure I could handle being on a little boat and paddling around in a sea kayak in ice water for a week.

But Pete never gave up. Finally, in 2007, I said yes. Even now, I'm not really sure why I gave in. Maybe Pete just wore me down. Or maybe, after decades of trying to control things, I decided it was time to let go.

Pete was thrilled and went into fast motion. Within 24 hours, he had booked everything: the boat, flights, ground transportation and a place where we'd spend our first night in a tiny town called Gustavus, about 40 miles from Juneau, on the Gulf of Alaska.

* * *

We met in the Seattle airport on a Saturday afternoon. Pete had flown in from Cincinnati. I had flown in from Myrtle Beach, where I had just spent a week on a family vacation. When I got there, I saw that Pete had sent a text message to tell me he was in the Seattle Tap Room in Concourse B.

Pete was a man of extremes. At times, he could drink a lot and drink fast. All told, we had a brief, seven-beer layover.

From Seattle, we flew to Juneau, another two and half hours north. The airport there is the size of a convenience store. We boarded an eight-passenger Cessna for the 20-minute flight to Gustavus.

We flew low the whole time. Just below, I saw rivers, lakes, lagoons, mountains and glaciers.

As we were about to land, I could finally see the bay. It was dark blue and narrower than I had expected. I'd seen rivers as wide. But it seemed to extend forever, separating and branching out through the snow-capped mountains, more like a web of rivers than a bay.

But what really got my attention were the glaciers. For some reason, I had always had trouble wrapping my mind around the idea of glaciers. As a city boy, I used to confuse them with icebergs.

Pete set me straight. He explained that icebergs are chunks of ice that break off from glaciers. Many are big, like the one the Titanic hit. Some are tiny, the size of ice cubes. All glaciers, though, are huge. Some stretch for hundreds of miles. They move slowly through the mountains and valleys, scouring the earth, always advancing and retreating.

Still, I had a hard time envisioning them. But then, from the plane, I saw them. They looked nothing like icebergs. They were a confluence of white, blue and grey. They looked like great tentacles, snaking through the mountain ranges like giant, frozen rivers. Some of them stretched beyond my field of vision, even at 5,000 feet.

"There it is!" Pete exclaimed, pointing down at the bay. "Isn't it incredible?"

Good Lord, it was breathtaking, the most majestic landscape I'd ever seen. But it looked wild and daunting too, and I wondered what I had gotten myself into.

* * *

We landed on a runway that seemed far too short, descended the shaky aluminum stairs to the tarmac and grabbed our duffel bags from the belly of the plane. We slung them over our shoulders and lugged them through the tiny airport to the parking lot.

From there, a van took us to the inn, 10 minutes away. As soon as we left, I knew I was in a very special place.

The land was flat and rolled out in grassy prairies in every direction, surrounded by tall, dark evergreens rimmed by low, blue-green, snow-capped mountains in the distance.

We passed a dozen houses, a few lodges, a school, a small general store, a library, two restaurants and a gas station with old-time, red pumps. The whole scene reminded me of one of those colorized 1930s westerns.

We pulled into the long driveway of an inn. It was large and white, two-storied, with a reddish-brown roof. I could tell from all the angles and windows that there were many rooms inside. The front lawn was 50 yards wide, and the grass smelled freshly cut. On one side stood a wall of towering, dark green fir trees. On the other, a rolling meadow of tall grasses and wildflowers.

Just beyond the meadow, extending behind the building, was a sprawling garden, with alternating rows of vegetables and flowers — pansies, fuchsia, petunias, carnations, marigolds, snapdragons, sweet-peas, poppies, lupines and geraniums — in waves of red, white, pink, lavender, blue, orange and yellow. I was surprised to see such a vibrant display of flowers in a climate so harsh.

A split-rail fence framed the back and one side of the garden, some of it covered by blackberry, raspberry and red currant bushes. The air smelled earthy and sweet, a blend of rhubarb, flowers and pines. Beyond the garden stood an orchard, whose trees marched single file into the woods at the base of a broad, low mountain, the backdrop to everything. It was a scene that was at once wild and tamed, natural and crafted.

The owners of the inn were gracious hosts. We ate well that evening. After dinner, we sampled the local craft beers at a small bar next to the kitchen.

Even though it wasn't dark yet — in July, the sun doesn't set in Alaska until about 10:00 — we were exhausted. So we headed to our rooms. I closed the curtains to block the early sunrise, then slipped into bed.

* * *

My alarm went off at 7:00, but the hearty scent of bacon, eggs and coffee had already roused me.

I had slept like a man who had traveled 3,000 miles on a beer-of-the-month-club trip the day before. Still, I was tempted to snooze a little longer. But then someone started banging on my door.

"Time for breakfast!" Pete shouted.

I just knew his goofy face was scrunched up against my door.

"Get up, Don! We've got to be at the dock in an hour."

I was just stirring some blueberries into my oatmeal when the other guests began to get up, go to their rooms and check out. Soon I was the only one left at the table. That was fine by me, since I was packed and ready to go.

I savored my oatmeal, buttered some toast, sipped my coffee and sat alone, facing two large windows along the back wall of the inn. The glass was thick — to withstand the harsh winters, I guessed. The garden flowers were brilliant in the morning sun, and they swayed in the breeze. And through the glass, awash with light, all the colors of the garden danced and blended together, like a kaleidoscope.

I remembered it was Sunday. It felt like a Sunday morning in church. I knew it was cool outside. But with the sunlight streaming in, the air in the dining room was warm, and I felt radiant.

I also felt grateful. I felt grateful for everything, including Pete, for his persistence, for being there and for the courage to have finally said yes.

* * *

We boarded our small ship at a place called Bartlett Cove and set out for six days and six nights on Glacier Bay. There were nine passengers and five crew members. Our boat would cruise the bay by day and anchor in quiet coves at night. Most days, we would go sea kayaking. Some days, we would hike.

Now, on the first day, it was time to kayak. There were six kayaks in all: five two-man kayaks and a single for John, our guide.

"Let's go together, Don," Pete said. "You take the front, and I'll take the back."

I knew what that meant: Pete wanted to be in charge. I knew Pete was an experienced kayaker. He owned a kayak and took it out on a small lake near his house.

I didn't have nearly as much experience kayaking. But I had done a lot of canoeing as a kid. And I had done a couple of triathlons with Pete. They included canoeing on the Little Miami River. I remembered he insisted on being in the back then too. We flipped our canoe about every mile.

"Are you sure?" I said.

"You worry too much," Pete replied. "Besides, we're wearing wetsuits."

Pete could be so confidence-inspiring.

"Hey, guys!" John yelled. "Don't go very far."

I'm glad he did because Pete had already started paddling away.

"John said to stay close," I said.

"Don't worry. I'm just getting us into position."

Pete liked to say that kind of crap, knowing it made absolutely no sense. I knew him, though. He just wanted to see how far he could go before John called us back.

"Hey, guys!" John yelled, as if on cue.

Pete stopped paddling. We glided to a stop.

I looked around. What had seemed big from the air, as we flew in yesterday, was now nearly too massive to take in.

Our boat had anchored in the middle of a narrow stretch of the bay. In front of me rose a glacier, stormy blue and powder white. It must have been 150 feet tall.

On the other side of the bay, behind us, stood a rain forest. The tall evergreens were covered with mosses and lichens. I could see wildflowers and the trunks of downed trees along the forest floor. Streams flowed like fingers out of the woods, trickling down the rocky shore through brown moss-covered boulders and into the bay.

Surrounding everything were mountains that rose thousands of feet and stretched farther than I could see. The bay itself seemed endless too, like the ocean.

And there we were, Pete and I, in the center of all this, sitting in a 16-foot plastic kayak, floating like a leaf on a pond, best friends, saying nothing, directing nothing, wanting nothing, just floating, immersed in a new world, a larger world, for a moment, this moment, together.

* * *

All six kayaks were now in the water. John reminded us to stick together. Then he pulled a large, expensive-looking Nikon camera from his kayak. He told us that in addition to being a tour guide, he was a professional photographer. He said he would be taking pictures all week.

With that, as a group, we headed toward an enormous glacier. The closer we got, the more ice I saw in the water. At first, it was in the form of tiny icebergs, no bigger than ice cubes.

“Grab one, Don,” Pete said, leaning over and scooping one up in his hand. “Taste it,” he said, popping it in his mouth and chomping on it like candy. “It’s the oldest ice cube you’ll ever see.”

I reached out and snagged one. The water was freezing. The ice cube was clear and slick, and I could see small stone particles and air bubbles inside. I licked it and put it in my mouth. But with all that debris inside, I decided against biting it. It tasted clean, though. I guess I was expecting it to taste like salt or dirt. I sucked on it for a minute, numbing my tongue. Then I spit it back into the sea.

We kept paddling toward the glacier. The icebergs were getting larger, some now the size of basketballs, others as big as cars. Some were square, some flat, some domed. Pete maneuvered us through them, the smallest ones bouncing off the sides of our kayak. Then, a few hundred yards from the glacier, John yelled, "Stop everybody!"

We all stopped paddling.

"Quiet," he said. "Listen. Just listen."

At first, I wasn't sure what he meant. Then I heard something popping, crackling, the sound echoing off the glacier.

"This glacier is melting," John told us. "Every glacier melts. But now they're melting faster than ever. That popping is the sound of air bubbles escaping from the ice. The ice is constantly melting, so that popping sound never stops."

Suddenly, we heard a much louder noise, like a clap of thunder. A huge chunk of ice had broken off the middle of the glacier in front of us. It slid down the face, leaving a cascade of snow and ice in its trail. The ice mass exploded into the water, creating a broad wave, which slowly rolled toward us.

I looked around for John. He shouted not to worry, it wasn't a "big one." He said to just point our kayaks toward the wave and ride it. Pete re-oriented us, and I had to back paddle hard to give us enough time to square up. The first wave was now just seconds away.

"Hold on, Don," Pete said. "Here it comes!"

I watched as the wave hit us straight on, then felt it go under our boat, rocking us, front to back. It was like riding a kids' rollercoaster

— except surrounded by about a million gallons of ice water. I pushed my paddle down hard against the top of our kayak to steady myself.

"Holy shit!" Pete shouted. "What a rush!"

"Thank God," I said, relieved we were still upright.

"I can't believe we saw calving on the first day," Pete said. "This is going to be a great trip!"

Everyone was hooting and hollering, and Pete and I hadn't flipped our boat. Maybe he knew what he was doing after all.

After checking out the glacier a bit more, but still at a safe distance, we all turned around and headed for the other shore. It was as lush as the other side was frozen, an old-growth forest of massive hemlock and spruce trees. They stretched up and down the shoreline as far as I could see — a rocky, jagged shore line, etched with inlets and coves.

For the next hour or so, we explored several of those coves. Along the way, we saw an astonishing array of wildlife.

We saw sea otters with brown fur, the size of puppies, floating on their backs, looking surprisingly carefree. We saw several bald eagles. Until then, I'd never seen even one. We saw dozens of puffins, which John called "flying potatoes." And near the shore, we looked down into the clear water and saw large red, blue, green, yellow and purple starfish.

Pete and I began to drift away from the others, toward the center of the bay. We hadn't strayed far, but far enough to make me a little uneasy.

"Pete, let's stay with the group," I said.

"I'm keeping them in sight," Pete said. "We're fine. You worry too much."

Maybe he was right. Maybe I was worrying too much. Pete had been there twice before. He did seem to know what he was doing, and he hadn't steered me wrong so far. I guess I just needed to learn to relax.

Then suddenly, Pete cried, "Look! I think it's a sea lion!"

Oh God, I thought. I turned around to see Pete. He was pointing ahead to our left. I pivoted back around, looked out and saw something big thrashing near the middle of the bay. It was less than 100 feet away.

"Let's go take a look," Pete said. I felt our kayak surge forward.

"Come on, Pete," I said. "Those things are dangerous."

"It's not going to bother us. It's busy. It's eating lunch."

As we got closer, I realized it was indeed a sea lion. It was huge. I guessed maybe 10 feet long and 1,000 pounds. It was dark brown, with black fins, a small head, thick neck, flat nose, long whiskers and bulging black eyes.

I stopped paddling, but Pete didn't. We inched toward the beast. I could see its mouth and its teeth: four long, curved canines in the front with rows of cone-shaped incisors behind. Suddenly, "sea lion" made sense.

It was indeed eating lunch. It had caught a king salmon. It probably weighed 30 pounds, but the sea lion tossed it high in the air, like a rag doll, tearing it apart. Blood and pieces of flesh and bone flew everywhere. With each toss, the sea lion would take another bite of the fish, its head snapping back, like a ravenous dog chomping on a piece of raw meat.

"Pete, stop," I said in a loud whisper.

Now we were only about 20 feet away, close enough even for Pete because he finally stopped paddling. We glided to a stop and just sat there, transfixed as the predator violently, powerfully devoured the last of its poor prey.

Then the beast looked at us, opened its mouth wide, made a deep, growling sound and slipped under the surface of the water.

"Hey, guys!" John yelled, breaking our trance. "Get back here!"

I turned around to see him. He and the other kayakers were 100 yards behind us.

Then I caught a glimpse of Pete. He was just sitting there, his paddle resting in front of him, with a big smile on his face. He was quiet. Pete was seldom quiet. I think he was happy. I think he was happy that we had just witnessed something wild and intense yet we hadn't kept our distance. I think he was happy that we had seen that glacier calve and ridden the wave. I think he was happy to have steered us through those icebergs. I think he was happy to be back in Alaska and showing me the ropes. And although he never said so, in that moment, I think Pete was very happy to be alive.

I was happy too. I was happy to be guided for a change, to let go, to give up control. I was happy to leave my familiar world behind and enter this mysterious new one. I was happy to unplug. I was happy that this adventure was just beginning. I was happy at the prospect of not shaving for a week. And, of course, I was happy that I hadn't just been eaten by a sea lion.

* * *

The next morning, we all shuffled into the galley for breakfast. John was sitting at the end of the table, drinking coffee.

As we all munched on bagels, John told us we would start our day by kayaking to Margerie Glacier. There, we would paddle to shore near the edge of the glacier and eat lunch. Then we would hike up a mountain that borders the glacier.

"If everybody's up for it, we should be able to climb about 2,000 feet and see out about 10 miles," John said.

Two hours later, we were climbing that mountain. The trail was steep, narrow and very rocky. The brush, tall grasses and bushes, was coarse and thick. The climb was a struggle, and we had to stop several times to rest. But at about 2,000 feet, we reached a plateau. There, we all stopped and looked out over the bay.

John was right: we could see for miles. In the bright sun, the bay looked like a giant mirror. Everything was reflected in it — mountains, forests, glaciers, even the sky. Everything was revealed in the water.

The air was cool, and the wind bore the scent of everything below us: trees, flowers, moss, salt water, ice. The fragrance of all these things rose up to meet us on the wind, and I closed my eyes and breathed it in.

For a moment, I did not feel separate from these things. I felt one with them and everything. I felt I had known this once, long ago — and that if I could be still and open, as I was at that moment, I could know it again.

* * *

That night, Pete and I lay awake for a while in our bunks. I told him about my experience on the mountain that day, about my feeling of communion with everything.

I thought he might laugh or start snoring. But he listened and said he had had a similar feeling himself, the last time he was in Alaska.

"I've never put it into words," he said. "But that's how I felt too. I brought that feeling home with me, and I thought I'd never lose it. But I did. Now, though, I'm feeling it again. You're right. When you really think about it, it all begins to blend together."

Pete stopped talking. I thought maybe he had fallen asleep.

"Pete?"

"Yeah."

"Thanks."

“For what?”

“For bringing me here, for not giving up on me. For this whole thing.”

“Sure. Good night, Don.”

“Good night, Pete.”

* * *

The next day, we “shot the arch,” a massive arched iceberg carved by water, wind and time in a cove of the bay. The parabola-shaped opening was probably 50 feet tall but only about 20 feet wide. The water pulsed through it, tons of water, suddenly constrained and channeled, crashing violently against the walls in 10-foot surges. When the water hit those walls, it sounded like thunder.

I could hardly imagine going through there in a kayak. But we all huddled around John in our kayaks near the entrance, and he told us how to do it. The trick, he said, is to stay in the middle, point your kayak toward the other end and just ride it.

“Don’t try to steer or even paddle,” he said. “Just get out of the way and let it take you. Watch me.”

Then without hesitating, he showed us how by going first. Once we saw him ride the crest of those waves straight through and come out alive, our spines stiffened. We all began lining up.

Still, I knew this was not like any kayaking I had ever done. I understood why John had made us bring a helmet that day. I fastened mine tight.

All week, Pete and I had kayaked together. Today, though, one of the crew members was my partner and another passenger was his. On one hand, I was sorry not to be with Pete. But on the other, I got to watch him shoot the arch.

Pete and his new bowman were both big men. But going through the arch, with their helmets on, bobbing wildly at the mercy of the waves, they looked like a couple of Fisher-Price little people in a toy boat.

Over the roar, I could hear their screams, echoing off the walls, screams of ecstasy, of pure joy, like children opening gifts on Christmas morning. Hearing that was as thrilling to me as my own turn through the arch.

As I shot through, there was Pete waiting, cheering me on, looking as happy as I had ever seen him.

* * *

Friday would be our last day of sea kayaking.

We dropped anchor at a place in the bay called Adolphus Point. John told us it was a popular feeding spot for humpback whales. They spent their summers there, "rebuilding their blubber supply," he said, after migrating 3,000 miles every year from Hawaii, where they mate and have babies.

We had hoped to see one, but at a distance — and from the ship! And yet here we were, Pete and I, watching breathlessly from our kayak as three humpbacks headed straight toward us.

Side by side, one by one, they dove under the surface of the water, then emerged, like giant pistons. As they did, they blew great puffs of misty spray into the air. Their exhaling made a gushing sound, like steam blasting from a locomotive. Their backs were mottled black. They were now less than 100 yards away.

John yelled to tap our paddles on our kayak. Of course! During our orientation the first day, he had told us to do this if we ever saw a whale so it would know where we were and not accidentally upend us.

I felt so small and vulnerable. My heart raced. I had no good options. All I could do was wait, tap my paddle and hope the whales would hear us.

Then all of a sudden, they were gone. Fifty feet away, the giant creatures disappeared.

"Where did they go?" I asked.

"Oh, shit!" Pete said. "I think they're under the boat!"

"Keep tapping!" John shouted.

Pete and I tapped our paddles furiously.

Then a whale burst through the surface of the water 10 feet in front of me. Boom! It must have been 50 feet long. I could have reached out and touched it with my paddle. Its skin was bumpy, like a cucumber. It had a small fin on its back. Barnacles encrusted the underside of its mouth. Its eye was the size of a baseball. It looked like a gigantic human eye, and it was staring right at me.

Whoosh! The whale blew its spray hard and high into the air. The sound was so deep I could feel the vibration. Spray rained down on us. It tasted salty and fishy, like sardines.

Then a second whale burst through the surface, just to our left. Boom! Then a third, just to our right. Boom! They formed a crescent around us. They were all blowing their spray into the air. We were soaked with it.

By now, it was clear the whales knew where we were, so Pete and I stopped tapping and just sat there and stared at them as they stared at us. They seemed content just to watch us and didn't come any closer. They hovered gracefully. I started breathing again.

There we were, the five of us together in a big ring in the sea. The whales began moaning, groaning, almost singing. Maybe they were communicating with each other, I thought. Or maybe with us.

A few moments ago, these animals had terrified me. But then, maybe out of desperation, I let go. And now, as I looked into their eyes, I was no longer afraid.

As Pete and I sat there, we didn't speak. We had entered a wordless place, a place of stillness, a sacred place.

At some point, we realized that our friends were cheering. They had seen it all. What we didn't know is that John had been taking pictures the whole time.

* * *

The next morning, after a late breakfast, our boat cruised into Bartlett Cove, where most of us had met just six days earlier. We were not strangers now, though, and we didn't want to say goodbye.

A van was waiting at the dock to take us to the airport. But for a few minutes, we all lingered, hugging each other.

We promised to stay in touch. We said we'd see each other again. But we knew that wouldn't happen.

And it never did. Five years later, suddenly and unexpectedly, Pete died of a massive heart attack.

* * *

I've given up trying to make sense of Pete's death. But the more that time passes, and the more my specific memories of him fade and blur, the clearer I am on how our friendship changed me, how it opened and expanded me.

For me, our Alaska trip was the flashpoint.

There, I learned to let go, to let someone else steer. There, I remembered we are all connected and that I am not really separate from anything. There, I came to understand that that which had once seemed so foreign and even frightening to me had now become a part of me.

I discovered these things in 2007 in Alaska with my friend Pete. He had waited a long time for me. He is waiting for me still.

But separation, I now know, is an illusion.

I close my eyes and see Pete, smiling in our kayak, chomping on a tiny iceberg, shooting the arch. I see him sitting in front of me on the plane, pointing down at Glacier Bay and saying, "Isn't it incredible?"

Swimming Lesson

Richard Lonigan, an utter failure, decided to end his sad life.

Early one evening, he drove to a big bridge. Just as he had started across the pedestrian walkway, Richard heard someone below him cry out.

"Help!"

Richard leaned over the railing and spotted someone in the water. He ran back and scrambled down the bank. Twenty yards out, a boy was drowning.

Richard dove in, grabbed the boy and managed to pull him to safety.

That night, Richard reflected on the fact that he'd never learned to swim, and he began to think about his life differently.

Saved

The homes in my neighborhood were built 50 years ago. Only one of the original residents still lives there. His name is Bill Harper. He lives three doors down.

Bill lives alone. His wife died last year. Until recently, I hadn't met him.

I don't know most of my neighbors. Until the pandemic, I wasn't home much. I'm in sales, and I used to travel four days a week. But with everyone hunkering down and hardly anyone flying, I've been working from home.

It's been strange. Before, I set up appointments and called on customers. Now I live on Zoom.

It's been a big adjustment. Not just the work. But where I work and even where I live. I feel like a stranger in my own house. My wife and kids are driving me crazy. They're noisy, and they're always interrupting me. I lock the door to my office upstairs, but they still manage to get in. Some days, I can't get anything done.

Lately, I've been taking walks just to get away. It's quiet in the neighborhood. With the pandemic, everyone's inside. I like that. No need for small talk.

A few weeks ago, I went out for a walk. I was walking by Bill Harper's house when I heard someone call, "Good morning."

I looked over and saw Bill sitting on his front porch. He was wearing pajamas and reading the newspaper.

"Good morning," I said.

"Beautiful day."

"Yes, it is."

I smiled, gave him a little wave and kept walking. I'd almost passed his driveway when he called, "Got a minute?"

I didn't want to be rude, so I stopped.

"Sure," I said.

"I've got a quick question, if you don't mind."

So much for my quiet walk, I thought.

I walked up his driveway. Bill got up and laid the newspaper down. He was tall and thin. I knew he was old. I'd seen him, driving by his house, many times. Now, close up, he looked even older. His face was drawn, and his pajamas hung on him like a farmer's clothes on a scarecrow.

As I approached, he pulled a face mask out of his pocket and put it on.

"Just to be safe," he said.

"Oh, yeah," I said, pulling my mask out and slipping it on.

We stood there, two masked strangers, looking at each other for an awkward moment. I wondered what he wanted.

“I’m sorry to bother you,” he said. “Do you know how to use Zoom?”

“Yeah.”

“Well, Carol has — had — a computer, but I really don’t know how to use it. I was wondering ...”

“Would you like me to show you how to use Zoom?”

“Yes. But if now’s not a good time ...”

“Now is fine.”

“Oh, good. Please come in. By the way, I’m Bill Harper.”

I climbed the two steps to his porch and gave him a gentle fist bump.

“I’m Matt. Matt Jenkins. I live a few doors down.”

“It’s good to meet you, Matt. I know you’re busy. I won’t take but a minute of your time.”

He turned around and pushed open his front door. I noticed this took some effort.

“Come in,” he said.

I followed him into the foyer.

“It’s right here,” he said, shuffling into the dining room.

Near the edge of the table was a laptop, a MacBook Air. It was open. A power cord dangled from the computer to a wall outlet. The morning sun through the windows filled the room with bright light. Looking around, I noticed a layer of dust on everything.

Bill pressed a button on the keyboard, and the screen lit up.

“I never turn it off. I’m afraid I won’t be able to turn it back on. I don’t know Carol’s password.”

“I see. Do you mind if I sit down?”

"Please," he said. "Would you like something to drink? Some coffee?"

"No, thanks," I said, sitting down.

He pulled out a chair at the end of the table and sat down too.

"I'd sit next to you, but, you know," he said.

"I understand. Do you happen to have a Zoom account?"

"No."

I set one up for him.

"I need to show you how to use it. Why don't you sit here?" I said, patting the seat of the chair next to me. It's okay. We're wearing masks."

Bill pulled out the chair and sat down beside me. He folded his hands in front of him on the table. I noticed they were trembling.

I showed him how to set up a Zoom meeting.

"Do you happen to know who you'll be meeting with?" I asked.

"Yes. My children and my grandchildren, I hope. I haven't seen them since before the pandemic."

"Have they come to visit?"

"No. They think it's too risky for me."

"I'm sorry. Well, now you should be able to see them."

"Thank you."

He was staring at the computer. I noticed his eyes were moist.

"Is there anything else I can help you with?"

"No," he said, getting up. "You've been most helpful."

I followed him to the front door. I stepped ahead and pulled it open.

"I can't thank you enough, Matt."

"You're very welcome, Bill. It was good to finally meet you."

I started to give him a fist bump, but he opened his arms and embraced me. Standing back, I saw tears in his eyes.

"Are you okay?"

"Yes," he said, wiping his eyes.

I wanted to know for sure he was all right but didn't want to embarrass him. So I wished him a good day and invited him to call me with any questions.

I walked back down the driveway and took off my mask. I had gone for a walk that morning to be alone. Now solitude seemed so lonely.

I decided not to continue my walk. I went home.

Together

John and Christine met in their twenties in a shoe store in Manhattan. From the moment their fingers touched over a single shoe, they knew they were destined to be together.

A year later, they pledged their lives to one another. Ten years later, still childless and weary of the big city, they decided to start fresh. For years, they had dreamed of Alaska. Now they ventured there by train to make a new home.

They had a cabin built on the shore of Auke Bay. From their front porch, they watched glaciers calving, great frozen endpoints, once liquid, breaking free and returning to their origin.

For 40 years, they lived there simply, quietly and happily. They both taught at the local campus of the University of Alaska until they retired. They were inseparable.

Then one November, Christine became ill, very ill. John brought her to doctors in Juneau, but they could do nothing for her, so he brought her home.

As the snow began to fall, John cared for Christine day and night, but she grew ever weaker. For each of them, the thought of losing the other was unbearable. In their suffering, they were fused.

In the spring, a neighbor went to their cabin to check on them, but they weren't there. Then he discovered a single set of heavy footprints in the soft soil from their front steps to the water's edge.

Who I Found in Angle Inlet

Angle Inlet is a secluded town, population 60. Technically, it's in Minnesota. But to get there, you have to go into Manitoba and then back south. Outside Alaska, it's the only place in the United States north of the 49th parallel.

Minnesota became a state in 1858. That's the year Jacques Bernard was born. He was born in Angle Inlet. There's a rumor he still lives there. I know that sounds crazy. But I'd heard that rumor all my life, and I had to find out for myself.

So I set out for Angle Inlet to see if I could find the oldest man on Earth.

* * *

I first heard the rumor as a boy, growing up in Minneapolis.

"That's right," my friend Greg said when we were eight years old. "He was born in 1858."

I was too young to do the math in my head. But I knew my grandfather was born in 1920 and he was now dead. I knew it was impossible for anyone born in the 1850s to still be alive.

“Bullshit,” I said.

“Yeah, bullshit,” said my friend Doug.

“How do you guys know it’s not true?” said my friend Greg.

“Nobody could live that long.”

“Yeah,” I said.

“Well, guess what?” Greg said. “Those guys in the Bible lived *hundreds* of years.”

“That’s a bunch of crap!” Doug said. “Those stories aren’t really true.”

“Yeah!” I said. “A bunch of crap!”

And so it went all through my childhood. Every once in a while, someone would say they’d heard yet another new rumor that a guy named Jacques Bernard, born before the Civil War, was living in a cabin in the woods in Angle Inlet.

By the time I turned 40, my life had become crowded and busy. I had a family, a wife and two kids. I had a big job with global responsibility. I traveled a lot. Between email and social media, I was almost always online. And wherever I went, it seemed CNN was breaking in with bad news. My life had grown frantic, heavy and rather predictable.

One evening, we were having dinner as a family, a rare feat anymore. My son Ethan mentioned that someone at school had told him about a very old man living in the woods in a place called Angle Inlet.

“What?” I said.

"Yeah, Dad. His name is Jacques Bernard. He was born before the Civil War."

"That's impossible," my wife said.

"I heard it too," my daughter Emma said.

I hadn't heard that rumor in a while. Maybe my life had gotten too busy or the din of my everyday existence had grown too loud. Now, hearing it again from my children made me think of my own childhood and how such a silly rumor had captivated me as a kid.

Thinking about that made me long for a simpler time. It made me want to take a break from my serious, grown-up life and chase down a fanciful, childhood dream.

* * *

I left my home in Eden Prairie, a suburb of Minneapolis, for Angle Inlet on a Saturday morning in early July.

"Please stay in touch," said my wife Melissa, sounding tentative.

"I will. I'll call you every day that I have cell reception."

"OK," she said, giving me a big hug. "But I hate the idea that you might be out of touch."

"Don't worry. I'll be fine," I said, as I gave Emma and Ethan a kiss and a hug.

But in truth, I wasn't sure about this trip. I mean taking a week off of work to find a guy who was supposed to be older than my great, great grandfather, living in a part of the world so remote that most residents of the state had never heard of it and so oddly situated that surveyors, mapmakers and government officials still had trouble deciding which country it was in.

I must be going through some sort of a midlife crisis, I thought.

But I had to find out, once and for all, if the rumor was true. So I got in my car, waved goodbye to my family and headed north on MN-89.

It took me nearly eight hours to reach the Canadian border. According to Google Maps, it should have taken me six. But every hour or so, I stopped to catch up on email and texts.

After clearing customs, I headed northeast along two different highways through the prairies of Manitoba. At some point, I lost cell reception. So I pulled over, pulled a map out of my glove box and spread it out on my passenger seat, the old-fashioned way.

Finally, I came to a sign that read "Welcome to the United States." In smaller type below, it said visitors must stop ahead at a place called Jim's Corner and report to customs.

Soon the highway became a bumpy, two-lane road. I spotted a small, wooden hut marked "Jim's Corner." I got out, opened the door and stepped inside. There in a booth was a videophone with two red buttons, one for visitors from Canada to call US Customs, the other for visitors from the US to call Canadian Customs.

I picked up the receiver and pressed the button for US Customs. A stern-looking woman appeared on the small screen in front of me. She asked my name, where I was from and where I was heading. Then she asked me to hold up my passport.

"Enjoy your stay," she said clinically.

I got back in my car. Now the road turned from paved to gravel. A few minutes later, I spotted a small sign that read "Welcome to Angle Inlet, Pop. 60."

I looked around and saw a few small, wooden buildings: a post office, a schoolhouse, a church, a general store. There were no other cars and only a few people walking around. *This must be downtown Angle Inlet,* I thought.

I had booked a cabin at Young's Bay Resort, near the edge of the Lake of the Woods, dubbed "The Walleye Capital of the World." It was just a few minutes away. I checked in and put my gear in my cabin, which I was happy to learn had WiFi.

Across the street was a place called Jerry's Bar and Restaurant. It was early evening, and I was hungry. I called Melissa to let her know I'd arrived, then walked across the street to get something to eat.

Jerry's was a long, gray, wood building. Hanging between posts along the front porch were two, big red and white banners with "Budweiser" along the top and "Welcome Fishermen" along the bottom. I climbed the steps and went inside.

The place was packed with guys wearing caps and fishing vests. Country music was blasting. Cigarette smoke hung thick in the air. On a widescreen TV, the Twins were playing the Reds. I didn't see an open table, so I took a seat at the bar.

"What can I get ya, buddy?" the bartender said.

"I'll start with a Budweiser. And could I see a menu?"

"Menu?"

"Yeah."

He looked down the bar at the other bartender.

"Hey, Debbie! You got a menu?"

"What?" she said, her eyes nearly shut against the curling smoke from her cigarette.

"A menu!"

"Yeah. Hang on," she said in a gravelly voice.

She stepped down to the end of the bar, near a window into the kitchen, and picked up what looked like a laminated sheet of paper. She stepped down our way and handed it to the bartender.

"Thanks," he said.

Debbie squinted at me and took a drag from her cigarette.

"Here you go," the bartender said, handing me the menu.

"Thanks."

I looked down at the menu. It was indeed a laminated sheet of paper with items printed by hand: hamburger, cheeseburger, fish sandwich, french fries, coleslaw, soup of the day and vegetable medley (seasonal).

A bowl of vegetable soup sounded good.

"What's your soup today?"

"Chili."

"How about the vegetable medley?"

"It's not in season."

"Okay. I guess I'll have a cheeseburger, french fries and coleslaw."

"Comin' right up," he said, taking the menu.

He walked over to the little window into the kitchen and yelled, "The special!"

Then he grabbed a bottle of Bud, popped the top and sat it down in front of me. He grabbed beers for a couple of other guys at the bar, then came back down to me.

"First time in?" he said.

"Yeah. It's my first time to Angle Inlet."

"Here to do some fishing?"

"No, not really."

"Camping?"

"No, I've come up from downstate, looking for somebody."

"Really? Who are you looking for, if you don't mind me asking?"

"I'm looking for a man named Jacques Bernard."

He looked at me, smiled a half smile and blew air out of his nostrils.

"You mean the oldest man on Earth?"

"Yeah! Do you know him?"

"I know a guy named Jacques Bernard. But he's not the oldest man on Earth."

"How old would you say he is?"

"Around 80."

Rumors morph. It's the nature of rumors. Maybe there's an old guy up here named Jacques Bernard whose great, great grandfather was born in 1858 or something like that. I must be crazy. And this bartender must think I'm crazy.

"Does he live around here?" I said, just trying to make polite conversation.

"Somewhere around here. I don't know where exactly. Somewhere out in the state forest."

"How do you know him?" I said, now wondering if I was being played.

"He comes in here two or three times a year. He sells us vegetables he grows on his land out there. You know, the vegetables for our medley."

Well, at least he knows a guy named Jacques Bernard.

"I see."

"Why are you looking for him?"

"Well, it might sound crazy. But I've heard that rumor about him all my life, and I decided to take a few days off and come up here and find out once and for all."

"Well, I'm sorry to tell you this, but I think you're wasting your time."

"Why's that?"

"You're not going to find him. And you're not the first fella who's come up here looking for him either."

"Food's up!" someone yelled from the kitchen.

"I'll be right back," the bartender said.

He sat my food on the bar.

"Ketchup?"

"Yes, please."

"Debbie! Bottle of ketchup!"

"Anything else?" Debbie said sarcastically.

"Yeah," the bartender said. "While you're at it, how about a napkin and some silverware too?"

Debbie grabbed a bottle of ketchup, a napkin and a fork from under the bar.

"Here you go, mister," she said, her cigarette bouncing up and down as she spoke.

"Thanks."

I opened the bottle and shook some ketchup onto my plate.

"I don't think I caught your name, young fella," the bartender said.

"My name is Jason," I said, extending my hand. "Jason Peterson."

He took my hand. His skin felt like leather.

"Dave. Dave Swanson."

"Good to meet you."

"Likewise."

"So this guy, Bernard. He lives in a forest?"

"Yeah, in the Northwest Angle State Forest, just south of here."

"But you're not sure where?"

"No, and there's a lot of land out there."

"Is there a trail into the forest?"

"Yeah. Several trails. But you're wasting your time if you think you're ever going to find him there. You'd be better off waiting until he brings us those vegetables."

"When will that be?"

"About two weeks."

"Well, I need to be home by Friday."

"Too bad."

"How far do those trails go?"

"I don't know for sure. I'd say about 10 miles. It's a big forest."

"How would I get to them?"

"Well, you'd drive back down the main road you came in on. A few miles down the road, you'll see the first trailhead on your left."

"How about the other trailheads?"

"Those trails are farther down the road. They're about a mile apart."

"So there's just three trails into the forest?"

"Well, there's another trail beyond those three. But you can't hike it."

"Why not?"

"It's on Red Lake Indian land. It's off limits to people like you and me."

"Got it."

"Another Bud?"

"Why not? I'm on vacation."

* * *

I got up early the next morning, put on hiking clothes and drove into town to buy food for the week. My cabin was equipped with a full kitchen. When I got back, I made myself a hearty breakfast.

Then I started packing for my hike. I grabbed my backpack and threw in a pair of socks, a T-shirt, a poncho, a compass, a flashlight, bug spray, bear spray, a water filter, a first aid kit and a couple of water bottles. I made a couple of ham and cheese sandwiches and stuffed them, a couple of granola bars and an apple in too.

I sat down and sent a text message to Melissa to let her know I'd be hiking all day, probably out of cell phone range, and that I'd call her that night.

I slipped on my backpack. It was light. I walked to my car and slid my pack onto the back seat.

I looked over at the lake. I could see a bunch of fishing boats on the water. A guy was backing his boat down a ramp into the water. Another was waiting his turn. *No wonder no one knows where Jacques Bernard lives. Angle Inlet is about fishing. Everybody here is on the water, not in the woods.*

I drove through town and back out on the main road. A few miles later, I saw a trailhead at the edge of the woods, just as Dave had said. I parked my car across the road. I grabbed my backpack, slipped it on and hit the trail.

It was mid-morning. I figured I'd hike for about three hours, then head back. That way, I'd be sure to get back before dark. I also figured six hours of hiking was about all I could handle. I ran on a treadmill a few times a week, but I was hardly in great shape. I hoped my 40-year-old body was up to the task.

Thankfully, the terrain was pretty flat, and the trail was clear. The forest was thick with spruce, birch, cedar and pine trees. I saw lots of birds, squirrels and deer.

At one point, I heard a noise through the trees that I thought was a deer. It turned out to be a moose. I had heard moose could be dangerous. I was ready to climb a tree. But the moose just looked at me, snorted and moved on.

It was getting hot. I made sure I stay hydrated. By noon, I had drunk both my bottles of water. I stopped at a creek and used my filter to refill them. I sat on a rock overlooking a small waterfall and ate a sandwich, a granola bar and an apple for lunch.

I pulled out my cell phone. No coverage. I thought about my family. I hoped they were all right. I thought about the emails that must be piling up in my inbox and the projects that would be waiting for me at work. I wondered what was happening in the world. I missed Google News.

I hiked on, deeper into the forest. Dave had said these trails go for about 10 miles. If the terrain stayed flat and the trails stayed clear, I figured I could make 10 miles in a few hours. Therefore, if Dave was right, I figured I should be able to cover all three trails in three days.

I kept hiking. I saw another moose but no people. I knew finding Jacques Bernard was a long shot. But I thought I might at least see other hikers. I guessed they were all fishing.

I wasn't used to being alone. At work, I was constantly interacting with other people. It felt strange to be alone. I felt a bit off-balance.

I looked at my watch. I'd been hiking for a little more than three hours. I decided to head back.

On my way back, I started thinking about work again. Once again, I began to wonder if this trip was really a good idea. I mean there was virtually no way I was going to find Jacques Bernard, and I was burning a week of my vacation. *I have to be going through a mid-life crisis.*

When I got back to my cabin, I showered, changed clothes and called Melissa. I checked a few email messages and scanned the news online. I was pretty tired and didn't feel like fixing dinner for myself, so I walked over to Jerry's.

Once again, the place was packed with fishermen, so I sat at the bar. I didn't see Dave tonight. Debbie was on duty. I ordered a Budweiser and the special.

"Sure thing, darlin," Debbie said with a little smile, the tip of her cigarette affixed to her bottom lip.

* * *

My second day of hiking, down the second trail, was much the same as the first, except today I passed a few hikers. I asked if they'd seen any cabins or anyone living in the woods. They said no.

I had a growing suspicion this was a wild goose chase. Yet I felt less regret about being there. As I had gone through my email the night before and scanned it again that morning, I had resisted responding to any of my messages. I knew hearing from me would send a bad signal to my employees about how they should be spending *their* vacations.

More than that, though, I realized that I really didn't need to respond. Either someone else would take care of the urgent stuff or it could wait until I got back. For the first time in years, I didn't simply react, and that felt good.

I found a stream and stopped for lunch. The day before, I had gotten back well before dark. So I decided to push it a little and hike for four hours before turning around, assuming the trail went that far. I found out it did.

As I hiked back, I felt tired. When I reached the stream where I'd had lunch, I decided to lie down on a bed of pine needles. I stuffed my knapsack behind my head.

I seldom took naps at home. I never had time. Now, though, I paid attention to my body. The breeze was cool on my face. Birdsong and pine filled the air. I closed my eyes and fell asleep.

When I got back to my cabin, I called Melissa. But I decided not to check email or go online at all. Instead, I took a shower and walked over to Jerry's for dinner again.

Dave was back tending bar. He asked if I'd seen Jacques Bernard yet. I told him no. He laughed and said I told you so.

We started talking about our families. We must have talked for an hour. Then I went back to my cabin. I opened a window, and the owls and nightingales sang me to sleep.

* * *

The next day, I made myself a big breakfast and took off for the third trail. I did not check email before I left.

I got an early start and decided to push it to see if I could hike five hours out and five back. I didn't know if the forest extended that far. But I figured this might be my last chance to find Jacques Bernard, and I wanted to give it my all.

In the early afternoon, I was just about to turn around when up ahead to my left I thought I saw a moose through the trees. I stopped. I squinted to get a better look. Whatever it was, it was big, and it wasn't moving. I kept walking on the trail. As I got closer to the object, I realized it was a cabin.

My heart was beating fast and hard. *Could I have found him?* Now the trail became overgrown with brush, as if it were a barrier. I took a deep breath and pushed ahead.

Twigs snapped beneath my feet. The front door of the cabin creaked open. I froze.

"Who's there?" came a disembodied voice from inside.

I was afraid. I didn't know what to say.

"I said, who's there?"

A figure appeared at the door, a man of slight build with long white hair and a long beard, wearing a brown shirt and overalls. He stepped out onto the porch. His hands hung empty at his sides.

"My name," I said in a trembling voice, "is Jason Peterson."

"What do you want, Jason Peterson?"

"I'm looking for a man named Jacques Bernard."

The old man stepped over to a rocking chair on the porch and sat down. The chair creaked loudly.

"Then I suppose you found him," he said.

I couldn't move. I remembered my friend Greg all those years ago talking about the old men in the Bible living hundreds of years. I wanted to see how old this guy was, but I wasn't sure I was welcome to come any closer.

"You just going to stand there all day, young man?"

Well, this is it. The moment of reckoning. I stepped forward on the trail until I was just short of the steps to his porch.

"Come on up," the old man said. "I don't bite."

Trying my best not to look afraid, I grabbed the railing and climbed the steps. When I reached the porch, the old man stood up and extended his hand.

"Jacques Bernard," he said.

"Jason Peterson," I said, taking his hand. It felt bony and frail.

"Pull up that chair over there," he said nodding toward the end of the porch and sitting back down in his rocker.

I picked up the chair, pulled it toward him and sat down.

Now I got a better look. His hair was wispy, his face a labyrinth of wrinkles and his clothes hung on him like a scarecrow. But his eyes were green and bright. I remember thinking he had the eyes of a child.

"So why are you out here, looking for me?" he asked, smiling. He was missing some teeth.

"Well, Mr. Bernard, I've heard a rumor about you for a very long time."

"Is that right? What kind of rumor?"

"Well, I know it sounds crazy. But all my life I've heard a rumor that you're the oldest man on Earth."

"The oldest man on Earth, eh? Well, I *have* been slowing down a bit lately," he chuckled.

"Mr. Bernard, if you don't mind me asking, how old are you?"

"How old am I? Well, let's see. My arithmetic is getting a little rusty."

"Well, what year were you born?"

"That I know, Mr. Peterson. I was born in 1858."

I expected him to say something else. Maybe like he was off by 80 years. But he just sat there with a small smile, gently rocking.

"Did you say 1858?"

"That's right. I was born right here in 1858."

"So that would mean you're 159 years old."

"I reckon so."

"But that's impossible!"

"Maybe for you. Maybe for most folks. But not for me."

"What do mean?"

"Do you mean how is it that I could live this long?"

"Well, yes."

"Come with me," he said, slowly pushing himself up on the arms of his chair. "I'll show you."

He turned around, pulled open the door to his cabin and shuffled inside. I got up and followed him.

The cabin was one big room. A ladder ascended into an opening in the ceiling. There was a bed in one corner. In the center of the room was a table with four chairs around it and an oil lamp on top. An open-faced cabinet held dishes, pots and pans, utensils and ceramic mugs. Three rocking chairs ringed the stone fireplace. Inside the hearth was a big, black pot, suspended by an iron arm anchored into the stone. Two kerosene lanterns hung from wooden rods extending from the walls. There was a bookcase against one wall, filled with books. Several windows made of thick glass let in scattered light. I saw no appliances or any sign of electricity.

"Back here, Mr. Peterson," the old man said, opening a back door and stepping through it.

I followed him out onto a back porch. Just beyond it was a clearing in the woods, about the size of a small backyard in suburbia. It was filled with light green meadow grass. In the center of the grass was a large, rectangular garden.

Tools of all sorts — a shovel, a spade, a mattock, a hoe, a bow saw, a rake — were neatly arranged along the back porch, leaning against the wall of the cabin.

"Let me show you my garden," the old man said, descending two steps, holding tight to the wooden railing.

I followed him down the steps and out onto a dirt path that led to the garden. The old man walked slowly but without assistance. When he got to the edge of the garden, he stopped and put his hands on his hips.

"Here, Mr. Peterson," he said, nodding toward dozens of neat rows of vegetables. "Here is your answer."

When I was growing up, my mother had kept a vegetable garden in our backyard. I used to help her tend it. We grew carrots, beans, tomatoes, lettuce, squash, peppers and corn. I saw all these here.

"I don't understand," I said. "This garden is the reason for your longevity?"

"That's right."

He stepped carefully between two rows of carrots, toward the center of the garden.

"Come," he said, beckoning me with his hand.

He took a few more small steps, then stopped and bent down slowly, his knees cracking. He grabbed the leafy end of a carrot and yanked it up.

"Here you go, Mr. Peterson," he said, standing up slowly and handing me the carrot.

"Thank you."

"You're welcome. Notice anything special about that carrot?"

I examined it, turning it over in my hands. I held it up to my nose and sniffed it.

"No, I don't. It seems like an ordinary carrot to me."

"Oh, but it's not! There are no other carrots like this grown anywhere in the world."

"What do you mean?"

"This carrot is the result of hundreds of years of cross-breeding. Part of it comes from the Red Lake Indians. Part of it comes from Southwestern France, where my parents were born. Part of it comes from Quebec, where they lived before settling here."

"Interesting," I said. "But it still looks like an ordinary carrot to me."

"And yet, Mr. Peterson, it is an *extraordinary* carrot."

"With respect, Mr. Bernard. How so?"

The old man turned and looked me in the eye.

"If you eat enough carrots like this, Mr. Peterson, or any of the vegetables grown in this garden, you'll double your lifespan."

I blinked in disbelief.

"How do you know?"

"Let me show you something, Mr. Peterson," the old man said. "Follow me."

He carefully stepped back out of the garden and made his way through the meadow grass, toward the back of the clearing. I followed him. As we neared the edge of the grass, I noticed a stream. When we were almost to the stream, I saw two large rocks. Something was etched in each of them.

"Here, Mr. Peterson. Take a look."

I stepped closer to the rocks. On the first one was etched: *Philippe Bernard, 1831-1970.* On the other: *Josephine Bernard, 1833-1979.*

I couldn't believe my eyes.

"These stones mark the graves of my parents."

I felt dizzy. I took a deep breath.

"Are you okay?" he asked.

"Yes. Mr. Bernard, would you like to talk?"

We went back to his cabin and talked for the rest of that afternoon. He told me about his life. He told me about his first memories, there in the Northwest Angle, long before Angle Inlet was established.

He was an only child. As a boy, his parents used to take him to Fort St. Charles. It was more than a fort. It was a settlement where people lived, gathered and traded.

The original fort was built by the French in the 1700s. But by the time Jacques was born, the British had taken over. More people in the area spoke English than French. Jacques grew up learning both languages.

His parents lived a simple life in the Northwest Angle, cultivating and tending their garden and fishing in the stream and occasionally the Lake of the Woods. They made their livelihood by selling vegetables.

Jacques' father had a horse. Several times a year, he would ride it to nearby towns to sell his vegetables and a buy a few things his family needed. When Jacques was about 10, his father began taking him along. Jacques told me he saw a telephone and an electric light bulb for the first time on one of those trips. They were still relatively new inventions.

"What was that like?" I asked.

"I had mixed feelings. Part of me was astonished, of course. But part of me wondered how these things would change my life. I couldn't imagine talking to someone in another city, for example. It made me worry whether I would still appreciate where I lived. My life was simple. I knew that. I wasn't opposed to technology. But I had grown used to the slow pace of my life, to rising with the sun and feeling the Earth in my hands and under my feet. When I saw a car for the first time, part of me was in awe. But part of me felt sorry for the driver because he could no longer feel the Earth. When I first heard a radio, I had a hard time imagining listening to someone's voice without seeing their face and not being able to talk with them. And television? Well, I just found that silly. I've been going into Angle Inlet for years to sell my vegetables. I've seen computers and cell phones there. Over the past few years, a lot of people have been too busy talking or typing on their phones to talk with me."

"We've all gotten pretty busy, I'm afraid."

He simply nodded.

"Did you ever think about moving away?"

"Oh, sure. Lots of times. But my parents depended on me. And like I said, I was happy here. It might seem simple to you, but I love tending this garden. I love to fish. I love the woods. I love to read. My mother taught me to read, and my father bought me lots of books. I read a lot. Every time I go into town, I buy a new book. I read the newspaper there too. It keeps me current."

"Do you ever get bored?"

"No, I don't. A long time ago, I learned not to think much about tomorrow, to just be thankful for today. Every morning when I wake up, I thank God for the new day. Every day, I walk in the woods. The trees, the animals, the rocks and streams, they're my friends. Every day, I thank God for these woods. They're teeming with life, and they change all the time. There's something new to see every day."

I remembered playing in the woods near my house when I was a boy. I too loved the woods. How I missed those days.

"Were you ever married?" I asked.

"No. I met a girl once down in Grand Marais. I was there with my father. Her name was Anna. I liked her, and I actually went back to see her again. I rode my father's horse. I guess I was about 20. But all she talked about was wanting to move to the big city. I had no interest. So I knew I couldn't make her happy. I never saw her again. I like women, just never found one to marry."

"That's fair," I said, smiling. "Mr. Bernard, you are, by any measure, an extraordinary man. You've seen more change than anyone on Earth. May I ask you something?"

"Of course."

"Is life getting better? I mean do you think the world is improving?"

He smiled and pulled at his beard under his chin. He looked over my shoulder, a faraway look, as if he were somewhere else. Then his gaze came back to me, and he looked me squarely in the eye.

"Do you know," he said, "I never had a real conversation with my father, not about the big things anyway. I'm not sure why. He just didn't seem interested in talking much. But he loved to listen. He bought me books. And not just any books. Take a look over there on those bookshelves. You'll find Shakespeare, Tolstoy, Proust, Dickens, Hugo, Hawthorne, Thoreau, Whitman, Twain, Joyce, Hemingway, Faulkner, de Saint-Exupery, Frost and the King James Bible. My father knew all those books by heart. But he didn't know how to read. My mother and I read to him. My father lived and died in this little place. But he was a man of the world. I do think the world is getting better, Mr. Peterson, because it's getting smaller. These days, anyone can become a person of the world. I just hope we don't forget the small things — the joy of walking in the woods, the wonder of watching a storm move in, the satisfaction of patiently watching a garden grow. I hope people don't forget how to listen to one another."

He paused and smiled.

"What about you, Mr. Peterson?" he said, folding his hands in front of him on the table and leaning forward slightly. "Tell me about your life."

I blinked, trying to absorb what he had just shared. Suddenly, my life seemed so superficial and boring.

"Well, I'm married. My wife and I have two kids, a boy and a girl, 10 and eight. I live in Eden Prairie."

"Where's that?"

"Near Minneapolis."

"Oh."

"I work for a big software company. Do you know what software is, Mr. Bernard?"

"I'm familiar," he said with a grin.

"I'm a vice president there, in charge of new business development."

"Sounds like a big job."

"It is. Some days, to be honest, maybe a little too big. I work every day. I travel a lot. And I see my wife and kids less and less."

"Not good," he said.

"No. Not good at all."

"Do you have a cell phone?" he said.

"Yeah."

"Doesn't work out here, does it?"

"No, it doesn't."

"How does that make you feel?"

"To be honest, I'm beginning to get used to it. I've been hiking out here in the forest for three days, and I'm beginning to get used to being out of touch."

"You mean you don't miss all that software stuff?"

"Not at all."

"What do you miss?"

"I miss my wife and kids."

He smiled.

"Are you hungry?" he said.

"Yeah. I guess I am getting hungry."

"You know, you'll never make it back to Angle Inlet tonight before dark."

"I suppose you're right."

"You're welcome to stay here."

"I'd be glad to, Mr. Bernard. If it wouldn't be an inconvenience."

"No trouble at all. You can sleep in my old bed up in the loft."

"Mr. Bernard, do you mind if I ask you something?"

"Go right ahead."

"Have you ever told anybody the things you've told me today?"

"No, I haven't."

"Why not?"

"It's simple, Mr. Peterson. First, when I go into town, everybody is interested in my vegetables. But they're all too busy to ask about me. To be honest, despite our conversation today, small talk is not my strong suit. Second, you're the first person who's ever visited me here."

"You're kidding. The first?"

"Yep."

"I wonder why. Hasn't anybody ever come by here?"

"Oh, I see hikers from time to time. But they never stop. Only you have ever walked up to my cabin."

"I'm glad I did."

"Me too. Now let's go get dinner."

We went back out on the back porch. He handed me a fishing pole and a small, wooden box filled with dirt. We walked through the meadow grass to the stream. He took the fishing pole and the box from me. He stuck his fingers into the dirt and pulled out a worm.

He baited his hook and threw his line into a shaded pool. A few minutes later, he pulled in a big rainbow trout.

"This should be enough for the two of us for dinner," he said. "Along with some vegetables, of course."

We stopped in the garden on the way back and picked several different vegetables. It reminded me of spending time with my mother in her garden. I untucked my shirt and used my front shirt-tail to carry the vegetables. It was something my mother had taught me when I was a kid.

"Clever," the old man said.

When we got back to the cabin, he asked me to go down to the stream to get a bucket of water so he could wash the vegetables and we could wash our hands and have fresh water to drink.

"And pick some blackberries while you're there," he said. "You'll see berry bushes down by the stream. We'll have blackberries for dessert."

By the time I got back, he'd cleaned the fish and was frying it in a big pan, which sat on an iron grate over a low fire in the fireplace. I helped him clean and cut up the vegetables, which he laid into the frying pan.

Over dinner, I asked, "Does this mean I'm going to live to be as old as you?"

He laughed.

"Not yet. I've been eating these vegetables all my life. I'm not sure how many you'd have to eat to double your lifespan. But I know it's a lot more than a helping or two. Otherwise, a lot of people in Angle Inlet and the people passing through there would be my age!"

After dinner, we talked by the fire. He told me how it was to hear about American boys dying in Europe in the first world war and how his parents simply couldn't believe him when he told them astronauts had walked on the moon. I told him about my travels around the world and how Apple introduces a new iPhone every year and how people line up to buy them.

We shared stories about our earliest memories growing up, about our parents tucking us into bed at night, about skipping flat stones on a pond, about sleeping under the stars in the summer.

"I guess some things don't change," he chuckled.

As I climbed the ladder to the loft, holding my flashlight in my teeth, I thought of Melissa and how I wouldn't be able to call her that night. I hoped she wouldn't worry.

* * *

I said goodbye to Mr. Bernard after breakfast the next morning. I'd given him a granola bar, the first he'd ever tried. He liked it.

He insisted I take a burlap sack full of vegetables. I carefully put them into my backpack.

"You know," he said, "it's not just those vegetables that have made me grow so old."

"What do you mean?"

"I think there's another reason too."

"What's that?"

"Except for a few times when I was being chased by wild animals, I don't move very fast. I go at my own pace. I've never owned a car or a radio or a TV or a telephone or a computer. I don't own anything that would make me go faster than I want to go. I wake up when the sun rises and go to sleep when it sets. Somehow, life slows down when you live at your own pace. You should try it, Mr. Peterson."

"I will."

"Good," he said, extending his hand.

"Thank you," I said, taking it.

As we walked onto the front porch, I turned to him.

"Mr. Bernard, I do have one last question."

"What's that?"

"There must have been a lot of other hikers out this way over the years. Why do you think I was the first one who stopped?"

"Well, let me ask you, Mr. Peterson. Why did you come out here?"

"I was chasing a rumor, I guess. I needed to settle a question that had been on my mind for as long as I can remember. I had to find out if you really exist."

"So you were curious."

"Yeah."

"Well, there's your answer, Mr. Peterson. People don't discover things because they follow the same path everyone else is on. They discover things because they're curious."

He sat down in his rocking chair.

"The world is still being created, Mr. Peterson," he said, his green eyes sparkling. "You and I are still being created. Stay curious. It's amazing what you'll find."

"Thank you, Mr. Bernard. I will."

As I descended his steps and started walking away, he said, "I suppose you'll be telling people about me."

"Only if you want me to."

"It's up to you."

"I'll think about it. I'm not sure anyone would believe me anyway."

"Take care of yourself, Mr. Peterson. Your family too. And don't forget to slow down a bit."

* * *

When I got home, the vegetables were still fresh enough to eat. But I didn't eat them. Instead, I dried them. I'm keeping the seeds to plant in the spring. Last fall, I tilled a garden in my backyard. Emma and Ethan helped.

Now I am waiting. I am waiting for spring. The snow outside is nearly a foot deep. I used to use a snowblower to keep my driveway clean. Now Ethan and I shovel a path to the mailbox. Usually, a snowball fight breaks out.

I've been working from home a few days a week. Melissa and I don't go out as much anymore. We've been spending more time together as a family. Sometimes, we hike in the woods.

I'm slowing down, spending more time with people and less time online. I walk every day just to feel the Earth beneath my feet. I started reading books again. I'm learning French. And I feel grateful for who I found in Angle Inlet.

Berries

As boys, he and his brother spent a week every summer in northwestern Pennsylvania, where their father grew up. The summers are short there. By July, the blackberry, raspberry and blueberry bushes which cover the wooded hillsides are heavy with fruit.

Their father would take them into the woods to pick berries. When their bushels were full, they would leave the cool woods and hike back in the warm sunshine through meadows of green and gold, back to the old house, where their grandmother would prepare bowls of mixed berries swimming in cream and sugar.

Those vacations were an adventure because, as boys, the brothers lived in the city, and there were no hills or meadows or berry bushes there.

Now they're grown men, and they live a thousand miles apart. Their lives are busy, and they seldom see each other anymore. Their grandmother is gone, and her house was sold long ago.

But every summer, they get together. They go to a local market and buy fresh berries. They bring them home, wash them and gently drop them into bowls. Then they pour cream over them and sprinkle them with sugar.

They sit down at the kitchen table, bring spoonfuls of berries to their lips and breathe them in. They open their mouths and close their eyes and let the sweetness and tartness of the berries dance on their tongues, and they go back to the hills of Pennsylvania, to their grandmother's house, to a slower and simpler time.

The Essence of Friendship

The tears in my eyes helped me see more clearly. From the middle of the church, I could make out the white pall draped over the casket, which was at rest in the center aisle of the church just before the Communion rail.

It was hard to think of his body in there. I tried not to think of it.

Instead, I thought of a day more than 50 years earlier, when I learned what it means to be a friend.

* * *

The four of us had climbed out on a flat rock as big as a patio atop the Continental Divide, the highest point in Glacier National Park. A warm, strong breeze bore the sweet fragrance of Beargrass and fir trees from the valley below. All was silent save for the wind.

We gazed down at a brilliant blue lake. It was surrounded by a crescent of gray mountains crowned with snow and laced with glaciers that stretched like great, white fingers as far as we could see.

"Have you ever seen anything so beautiful?" Jimbo said.

“Not even close,” said Wags.

“Good lord,” I said.

“Amen,” said Frazier.

We stood there a minute or two longer, saying nothing more, watching the wind sweep glistening ripples across the lake far below.

Then Jimbo, tall and broad, slipped off his backpack and pulled out four sack lunches.

“You think of everything,” Frazier said.

Frazier was short, thin and bespectacled, with a shock of red hair.

“I try, Frazier,” Jimbo said, handing out the lunches.

The day we met, nearly 15 years earlier, we’d all given each other nicknames, which had stuck. Jim Davis was Jimbo, Bob Wagner was Wags, Bill Frazier was Frazier and I was Andy, short for Anderson.

Wags, Frazier and I sat on the big rock and dug into our lunches. Jimbo was still standing. He was looking down at us and smiling. I knew he was proud to have brought us up there. He had loved Glacier since he was a boy, when his father took his family there on vacations. He called it God’s country. He’d told us about it over beers the day we met, as freshmen in college.

“I’ll take you there one day,” he said.

At last he had. Now we finished our lunch and stretched out on the rock, basking in the warm sunshine and feeling on top of the world.

We had seen mountain goats in the distance on the hike up. Now one wandered over to us. It was bigger than a Saint Bernard with long, creamy white hair and formidable black horns. It boldly lept onto the rock where we were sitting. I had never seen a mountain goat so close. Its eyes were brown with horizontal, rectangular-shaped pupils. They looked demonic.

Frazier stood up. The animal looked at him but didn't move. Frazier had eaten his apple down to the core, and he tossed it to the goat.

"Don't do that," Jimbo said.

The goat bent down, snatched up the apple core and devoured it in one gulp.

"Oh, Jimbo," Frazier said. "You worry too much. Look how happy he is."

Frazier stretched out his hand. Apparently, the goat took it as a sign of aggression because it lowered its head and charged Frazier, goring him in his right thigh with its right horn.

Frazier cried out, his scream piercing the air and echoing in the canyon.

"Holy crap!" Wags shouted.

The goat twisted its head back and forth, trying to break loose, but only managed to dig its horn in deeper. The goat was stout, much heavier than Frazier, who was screaming like a man being tortured.

Jimbo jumped up.

"You son of a bitch!" he yelled, going for the goat.

The animal, dwarfed by Jimbo, backed off. In the process, it pulled its horn free.

Frazier shrieked and waved his arms wildly in the air. He began to fall backward, but Jimbo caught him. The goat let out a loud bleat, turned tail and bounded off.

Frazier moaned loudly, pitifully.

By now, I was at his side. He was sitting with his legs outstretched, as Jim held him under his arms. Blood was spurting from his thigh. A bright red pool began to form on the grey rock beneath him. I knelt down. The knees of my pants were instantly soaked with Frazier's blood.

"Lay him down on his back, gently," I told Jimbo.

My years as a surgeon and an emergency room doctor before that had steeled my nerves.

Jimbo eased Frazier back, cupping the back of his head in his right hand. I bent down to get a closer look at his thigh.

"Help me, Andy," Frazier said, looking up at me like a frightened child. "Help me."

"I will, Frazier. Don't worry."

By now, Wags was kneeling on the other side of Frazier. The sight of blood had always made him queasy, and he tried not to look down. He wasn't sure what to do, how he could help. He pulled his handkerchief from his pocket and wiped the sweat from Frazier's forehead.

I bent down to check out Frazier's leg. The top of his right pant leg was soaked with blood. There was a tear where the goat had gored him. Blood pulsated through the opening in the fabric. I knew I needed to stop the bleeding.

"Frazier, this is going to hurt," I said. "But I have to put pressure on your leg to stop the bleeding."

"Okay," he said, wincing.

I pushed down on his leg with both hands.

"Ahhh!"

"It's okay, Frazier," Wags said, rubbing his shoulder.

I turned to Jimbo and said, "Do you have a knife?"

"Yeah," he said.

"Oh, Andy," Frazier moaned.

"Don't worry," I said. "I'm just going to cut your pants open. I need to see that wound. I won't hurt you."

"Hold his head," Jimbo said to Wags.

Wags slid his hand under Frazier's head. Jimbo pulled a pocket knife from his pants pocket, opened it and handed it to me.

I took my hands off Frazier's leg. My palms were covered with blood. I wiped them on my thighs.

With my left hand, I pinched the top of the front of Frazier's right pant leg and pulled it away from his leg. I pierced the fabric with the point of the knife and cut it down to the edge of the tear. Then I pinched the fabric just below the tear, pulled it out and kept cutting all the way down, careful to keep the blade away from skin.

I laid the knife down and gently pulled back Frazier's now bisected pant leg, exposing the wound. Blood was streaming out. I put my hands over the wound and pressed down again.

Once again, Frazier screamed.

"I'm sorry," I said.

"It's okay," Frazier said through clenched teeth. "Am I going to be okay?"

"Yeah," I said. "You're going to be okay."

I had no way of knowing that for sure, but I wasn't about to add to Frazier's trauma by revealing my own uncertainty.

I looked up at Wags, who was still holding his hand under Frazier's head.

"Wags, take your jacket off, ball it up and put it under his head," I said.

"Okay," Wags said.

He looked over at Jim.

"Take his head for a minute."

Jimbo slid his hand under the back of Frazier's head again. Wags pulled off his jacket and rolled it up. As he was stuffing it under Frazier's head, I looked up at Jimbo.

"Do you have a first aid kit in that backpack?"

"Yeah," Jimbo said.

He got up and grabbed his backpack.

"I need a bandage," I said.

Jimbo reached into his pack, pulled out a metal box and opened it. Inside he found a large roll of gauze. He held it up.

"This?" he said.

"Yeah. Unroll it. The three of us are going to wrap it around his leg."

I took my hands off of Frazier's thigh and wiped them on my shirt.

"Hold the end," I said to Jimbo.

Jimbo held the end of the roll, as Wags and I took turns wrapping it around Frazier's thigh. We wrapped it around several times, until the bandage ran out.

"Now I need something bigger to wrap around the bandage — a shirt or a jacket," I said.

Jimbo pulled off his jacket.

"Okay," I said. "Lay that out and fold it over on itself. Make it as long as you can and about a foot wide."

Jimbo and Wags laid the jacket down on the rock and followed my instructions.

"Good," I said. "Now let's wrap that around the bandage."

The three of us did that together.

"Now we need something to snug it up," I said. "Jimbo, give me your belt."

I wrapped his belt around Frazier's leg a couple of times, crisscrossing it, pulling it snug, but not too tight, then tucked the buckle under the belt to fasten it as securely as I could.

"We need to get him to a hospital," I said.

"How are we going to do that?" Wags said.

"Wags, you'll run back down to the visitors center and have the ranger call for an ambulance. Jimbo, you and I will carry Frazier down there."

No one moved. I looked at Wags and said, "Go!"

Wags got up and started running down the trail.

"Jimbo, we're going to have to figure out a way to carry him."

"We can't do that," Jimbo said.

"What do you mean?"

"It's too awkward for the two of us to carry him, and we might hurt him. I'll carry him, Andy."

Jim was six foot four and weighed 220. At 33, he was still as strong as a horse, even without the lower half of his right leg, which he'd left in Vietnam. But the two-mile trail back to the parking lot was winding, uneven and steep. I wasn't sure this was a good idea.

"Are you sure you're up to this?"

"Yeah," Jimbo said. "Help me lift him."

Together, Jimbo and I scooped Frazier up until he was securely situated in Jimbo's arms.

"Are you sure about this, Jimbo?" Frazier moaned.

"Frazier, have I ever let you down?"

"No. I hope you won't start now."

"Grab my backpack," Jimbo grunted as he started down the trail. I grabbed his pack and scrambled to catch up.

Jimbo moved fast. Many times, he nearly lost his footing. I stayed close to steady him.

We passed hikers, coming up, along the way. They asked if they could help, but there was nothing they could do.

About halfway down the trail, it changed from gravel to a boardwalk made of thick wooden beams.

"I need to rest," Jimbo said.

"Give him to me," I said, dropping the backpack.

Jimbo lowered Frazier into my arms. He was too heavy for me to hold him very long. I laid him down on the boardwalk as gently as I could.

Jimbo plopped down on a step. He put his elbows on his knees, leaned forward and rested his head in his hands. I kneeled down over Frazier to inspect our makeshift bandage. Thankfully, the bleeding had stopped.

Jimbo pulled his canteen out of his pack and brought it over to Frazier. He helped him sit up with one hand and lifted the canteen to his mouth with the other.

When Frazier was finished drinking, Jimbo handed the canteen to me. Once I'd taken a drink, Jimbo took the canteen, tilted his head back and took great gulps, water spilling over his cheeks and down his neck.

Then he said, "Let's go."

Together, we picked Frazier up and put him back in Jimbo's arms.

Although the boardwalk was the smoothest surface along the trail, it was the hardest for Jimbo because he had to keep stepping down each descending section and, because he was holding Frazier, he had a hard time seeing his feet. So whenever Jimbo came to a step, he stopped, and I grabbed his arm to steady him and help him down.

Finally, the boardwalk came to an end, and the trail became gravel again. At that point, we had less than a quarter of a mile to go. Jimbo was breathing hard and drenched with sweat, but he kept going. As we approached the visitors center, Wags sprinted up the path to meet us.

"An ambulance is on its way," he panted. "It's coming from Kalispell. It should be here soon."

"Good job, Wags," I said.

Jimbo carried Frazier past the visitors center and down the steps to the parking lot. Wags and I were at his sides, but he took the steps slowly and didn't need our help.

The ambulance still hadn't arrived. Jimbo stood in the parking lot, holding Frazier.

"You can put him down now," I said.

"I've got him, Andy," Jimbo said calmly, his eyes fixed on a mountaintop in the near distance.

A few minutes later, the ambulance pulled in. Two paramedics got out and took Frazier from Jimbo. They put him on a stretcher and lifted him into the back of the ambulance.

I told them I was a doctor and asked if I could ride with Frazier. They said yes, and I climbed in.

"We'll follow you," Wags called after me.

"Okay," I said.

As we pulled away, I looked out the back window and saw Jimbo kneeling on the pavement. Wags was standing next to him with his hand on Jimbo's head.

In the back of the ambulance, a paramedic unwrapped Frazier's leg and redressed the wound, which was still oozing blood. Even the slightest touch of his thigh made Frazier call out.

He grabbed my hand and looked up at me. His face was filled with pain and fear.

"Can you give him some morphine?" I said to the paramedic.

"Yes," he said.

He gave Frazier a shot, and he began to relax almost immediately.

"You're going to be okay," I said.

"Thank you for being with me, Andy," he said, looking into my eyes and squeezing my hand before falling asleep.

It took us an hour and a half to get to the hospital. The emergency room doctor on duty was waiting. I explained I was Frazier's friend and a surgeon in Chicago and asked if I could join for the surgery.

"Okay," he said, looking me over.

With a four-day beard, I guess I didn't look much like a doctor. I'm surprised he didn't ask to see my license.

A nurse helped prepare Frazier for surgery. I put on a gown and a mask and scrubbed up. The emergency room doctor administered a general anesthesia, and we got to work.

Getting a clear look at Frazier's wound under the operating room lights, I realized it just how extensive it was. Muscle, veins and arteries were torn. It took the two of us four hours to knit Frazier's thigh back together.

I was sitting next to him in post-op when he began to come to. He looked over at me.

"Am I okay?" he whispered.

"Yes," I said. "You're going to be fine."

He closed his eyes and smiled. Then he opened his eyes and reached out his hand. I took it.

"Thank you for being with me, Andy."

* * *

"We are now honored to hear from dad's longtime friend, Doctor John Anderson," a woman said from the lectern.

I slowly rose to my feet and, leaning on my quad cane, stepped out into the aisle. My hand was shaking. A young man sitting across from me got up and stepped over.

"May I give you a hand?" he said in a loud whisper.

"I'm okay," I said with a smile. "Thank you."

I made my way up the aisle. When I got to the casket, I stopped and placed my right hand on the pall. I closed my eyes and stood there for a moment. I thought of Frazier and Jimbo and Wags too. They were all gone now.

I had prepared remarks. They were folded and tucked into the inside pocket of my suit coat.

But then I heard a voice in my mind say, "Speak from your heart."

I opened my eyes. I carefully stepped up into the sanctuary and made my way to the lectern.

I looked out at all the people gathered, but I could see only Frazier, lying not in his casket but on a stretcher, looking up at me as we bumped and zigzagged our way down through the mountains, squeezing my hand and saying, "Thank you for being with me, Andy."

I reached out to him with my right hand.

"Thank you for being with me, Frazier," I began.

The Clearing

He stopped walking and turned around full circle, searching the trees in the fast-fading light for a clearing or a way out. But there was no clearing, no trail, no end to the woods. With darkness falling fast, he began to realize that soon he would be able to see nothing at all.

His name was David, and he was 12 years old. He had explored these woods countless times but almost always with Matt, his older brother, or friends. He had never ventured this far.

School had let out early that afternoon, and Matt wouldn't be home until after football practice. His parents would be late. Once again, he and Matt would make their own dinner, usually macaroni and cheese or some frozen meal popped in the microwave, and watch ESPN as they ate. Sometimes Matt would take his food up to his room. He could hardly remember the last time they had had dinner together as a family.

With a few hours to kill, he sat at the kitchen table, eating a bowl of Frosted Flakes, staring out the back window.

He thought about texting a friend, maybe getting together to play video games. But then he dismissed the idea because he knew that would mean riding his bike nearly two miles, mainly on rough roads. He knew he could handle it. The problem would be on the way home. It would be getting dark, and his father had forbidden him from riding his bike that late in the day.

He couldn't invite anyone over because none of his friends' moms would let their sons visit without an adult at home. All these moms had two things in common: they all had 12-year-old boys; and they were all, therefore, suspicious of 12-year-old boys.

More and more, David found himself alone. He could find ways to fill the time but not the space. He felt empty. And his emptiness was caused not by an absence of things but affection.

Now, in the early afternoon, he sat alone in his kitchen and watched big, gray clouds move in. The temperature was in the low 40s, warm for Maine in early December. But there was a chill in the air, and the wind was kicking up. It blew through the tall trees at the edge of the woods that bordered his back yard. The sun, already low in the sky, cast shadows across the faded red and yellow leaves that covered all but small patches of pale grass.

David was learning to live in solitude. But there is a fine line between solitude and loneliness, and today he was feeling lonely. As he listened to the wind and watched the trees sway and the shadows dance and thought about the prospect of another afternoon alone, he felt drawn to the comfort and the company of the woods.

The woods had always been there for him. When he was very young, his father used to take him and Matt for hikes. His mother packed their lunch in a big brown bag: peanut butter and jelly sandwiches, apples and cookies. His father carried the bag and a thermos of chocolate milk in a small knapsack.

They would stop along the trail when they found a stump they could use as a table. They would sit together on a log, eating, taking turns drinking chocolate milk from the red cap of the thermos and reveling in their manly adventure.

As the years went by, though, the three of them took fewer hikes together. His father always seemed to have something else to do — work, some project, going out with his friends, even taking a nap. Eventually, the boys stopped asking him to go.

But David and Matt kept hiking. Not only that, they kept venturing deeper into the woods.

One day, they hiked all the way through the woods to a meadow of tall grasses and wildflowers which sloped down to a river. It looked like paradise. As the brothers ran down to the river, David felt special. He had helped discover a treasure.

After that, David and Matt would hike to the river often. Sometimes they would bring their fishing poles. Matt taught David how to set his line and fish. Sometimes they would spend an entire day there.

Sometimes they would bring a friend or two along. The trail to the river had become familiar to them, but to their friends, it was new.

David loved watching his friends experience it all for the first time. He especially loved when they got to the "reveal" of the river. Seeing it for the first time, his friends would always be astonished. David would look up at his brother, who would be beaming. Matt looked like a king, and David felt like a prince.

These were his favorite memories. And even though Matt no longer went hiking with him, the woods continued to give David comfort. In a way, they had become his best friend.

Now, on that blustery afternoon, he decided to go for one more hike.

* * *

David zipped up his coat and pulled down a red wool cap over his short brown hair. He eyed his gloves but decided against bringing them. If it got cold, he could keep his hands in his pockets.

He went out the back door and kicked a path through the thick layer of leaves and twigs across the lawn. At the edge of his yard, a dirt trail led into the woods. It was damp from a light rain the day before but not muddy. That was good because he was wearing his new Chuck Taylors. If they got muddy, his mother would be upset.

With the sun so low, the woods were darker than he expected. For a moment, he thought about going back to get his flashlight. But he would be home before dark, and so he decided to keep going.

David stepped into the woods. The air was heavy with the scent of wet leaves, and the trail felt cold under his feet. He hadn't been there since the hardwood trees had gone bare.

Everything looked so sparse now. This was good, though, because it meant he could see farther. He would need that because the sky was now overcast and, even without their leaves, the trees shrouded the dying light.

It was more than a woods, really. It was an old-growth forest, filled with a broad array of trees: aspen, birch, red and sugar maples, oaks, white and red pines, balsam fir and spruces. His father said he had moved there to be near "a wild place." This was indeed a wild place. David had seen many deer in these woods. Once he had seen a red fox. Matt told him there were even mountain lions.

The prospect of wild animals might have given David pause about hiking into the woods alone so late in the day. Once he would have found it too scary. But his life had become too routine, too predictable, too safe. And now it was the mystery, the not knowing, that drew him in.

He was also glad to get out of the house. For him, it had become such a cold and empty place. He knew Matt would come home and barely acknowledge him.

He had been this way since he started high school. These days, Matt ignored just about everyone. All he cared about was sports and going online. He spent hours in his bedroom. Their mother would sometimes scold him for spending too much time watching TV or on his computer and not enough time on his homework. She used to try to limit his TV and computer time. But it never worked. Besides, she wasn't around enough anymore to know what either of her sons was doing.

Now David came to a split in the trail. He had been there many times. He had always gone to the right.

To the right, the trail went on for another mile or so and led to the river.

To the left, it stretched for several miles. Matt had told him it led to a clearing and "civilization," although he had never actually gotten that far himself.

One day, as they came to the divide, David suggested they take the trail to the left.

"No way," Matt said.

"Why not?"

"We're not sure where it goes."

"But you said it leads to a clearing."

"That's only what I've heard. I've never been there. And even if it's true, it's way too far for you."

"Okay. Then I'll go there by myself."

"Don't even think about it," Matt said. "You'd get lost. You'd never make it."

For the moment, David backed off. But that longer and more dangerous trail continued to intrigue him, and his brother's dare stuck with him.

Now he stood at the divide and thought about Matt, the brother he had idolized growing up, the brother who used to show him the way, the brother who no longer wanted anything to do with him.

He stood at the divide, thinking about all these things, and stepped to his left.

* * *

David's parents were seldom together these days. They left for work and got home at different times. They ate their meals separately. They slept in separate bedrooms. And when they were together for any length of time, they argued. He didn't know which was worse, the silent tension or the fighting.

It wasn't always this way. He remembered his father kissing his mother on the cheek when he got home from work. He remembered them sitting on the couch together. He remembered them laughing together, talking together.

Sadly, those were distant memories now. These days, his parents barely spoke to one another. They no longer even called each other by name. David wasn't sure why they had drifted apart. But he knew exactly when they began to fight.

It was one of his earliest memories. When he was five, his father had taken him to a department store. They were in the toy aisle.

David was drawn to a red, plastic truck with big, knobby tires. He reached up on his tiptoes and took it off the shelf. It was so heavy that he had to use both hands. He set the truck down on the linoleum floor, rolled it back and forth and pushed it down the aisle as hard as he could. The rubber tires made a whirring sound. The truck hit the bottom of a metal shelf and bounced off. Cool!

"Hey, Dad!" David said. "Can we buy this?"

But there was no answer. He looked up. His father was not there. He walked to the end of the aisle, but his father was not there either. He felt a pain in his stomach. He dropped the truck.

David ran to the next aisle and peered down it. He saw strangers, but not his father.

"Daddy!" he called, now running past every aisle.

But there was still no answer.

"Daddy!" he screamed.

Then he stopped. He was out of breath, and he started to cry.

The whole thing was now like a bad dream. He could no longer remember exactly how he got to the customer service desk. He could only remember telling the lady there that his name was David, then hearing "Would the father of a little boy named David please come to the customer service desk?" on the loudspeaker.

Then he saw his father running towards him. At first, David almost didn't recognize him. His eyes were wild, and his normally stoic face looked pained and distorted. But then his father saw him. Tears ran down his cheeks. His father called him by name and, for the first time David could remember, he grabbed him and held him close.

They talked in the car on the way home. How did it happen? They figured that his father had stepped away for only a moment, while David was playing with the toy truck. And when they couldn't find each other, they headed in opposite directions. So the more they searched, the more they got separated.

It seemed to make so much sense in the car. But it all fell apart when they got home. His mother blew up.

"How could you be so stupid?"

His father had no defense. But rather than take it, his father gave it right back.

David no longer remembered what either of his parents said that day. He just remembered them yelling at each other into the night.

And he remembered how, after that, nothing ever seemed the same again. His parents never exchanged another happy word. They became cold and distant, initially toward each other and eventually toward their sons too. His family seemed to break apart, a "family" only in that they were all still living in the same house.

If only he had left that truck on the shelf. If only he had only stayed with his father. If only he had not upset his mother, none of this would have happened.

* * *

David had been walking for well over an hour now. Matt had been right. This trail was tough.

A tree trunk had fallen across the first creek he came to. The water was at least five feet below. But the tree trunk was wide and sturdy, and David was able to step across it without a problem, even looking down at the water rushing by.

Soon he came to a second creek. A fallen tree stretched across it too. But it was much thinner, and the creek was probably 10 feet below. He stepped onto the tree and felt dizzy. So he climbed down and made his way to the narrowest part of the creek. He decided to cross there.

Four rocks formed a jagged line through the water. The middle two were nearly submerged. None of the rocks was big enough for both of his feet, so he had to balance himself, one foot on one rock at a time. He got halfway across. His right foot was on the second rock, his left foot on the third. Only one more rock to go. But he slipped and he fell into the stream, landing on his hands and knees.

The stream was shallow, but he was soaked. The water was so cold it stung his skin. He jumped to his feet and sloshed through a ripple of water to the shore. There he faced a steep bank. There was no way around it, only up. So he grabbed onto small trees and roots in the earthen hillside to pull himself up.

He stood on the bank, shaken by his fall and now beginning to tremble from being cold and wet.

Between the heavy brush and the fading light, the trail was now nearly impossible to see. He drew a deep breath and tried to collect his thoughts. He guessed he was now easily more than halfway to the end of the trail. Maybe he could make it to the clearing Matt had told him about. For sure, if he turned back now, he would never make it home before dark.

He decided to go on.

* * *

Just a week earlier, his mother had picked him up after school to go shopping. He was not used to seeing her so early in the day. But she'd gotten off work early and needed to do some Christmas shopping. So she texted him and told him to meet her as school was letting out.

They drove to Rike's. It was a sprawling, ancient department store, known for its elaborate Christmas displays. It took up a whole city block. Some people drove hundreds of miles to shop there at Christmas. Some came just to see the displays.

Holly, tinsel and fake snow adorned every aisle. Christmas music and the smell of popcorn filled the air. Of course, Santa was there, receiving a steady stream of happy and frightened children.

David remembered his parents bringing him and Matt there as boys. They loved seeing Santa. Now his mother walked right past the big man, seeming not to notice.

"You need new tennis shoes," she said. "Come on."

She made a beeline for the kids department. His mother always walked fast when she shopped. He had to quicken his pace to keep up.

In the boys' shoes section, there were lots of great options. But he knew what he wanted: Chuck Taylors. Red ones.

"Are you sure?" his mother said. "And red?"

"Yes, Mother."

"Okay. I guess you know what you want."

He asked the clerk if he could wear them home.

"Absolutely," she said, smiling and putting his old shoes in the box. "Of course, you know, you'll now be the coolest young man in the store."

"Thanks," David said, smiling.

He stood up and began to walk around. He loved the feel of new tennis shoes.

"Let's go," his mother said.

David wasn't sure where they were going, but he followed his mother closely as they made their way through the crowded store. Then he remembered Rike's had an old-fashioned soda fountain. It was in the corner of the store, right where they were heading!

He and Matt used to like to sit at the counter and watch the "soda jerk" make milkshakes. His parents had to lift them up onto the tall, red vinyl, swivel bar stools. Now David grabbed the edge of the counter and hoisted himself up.

He expected his mother to sit down beside him. Instead, she took a $20 bill out of her purse and laid it on the counter.

"Order yourself something," she said. "I'm going to do some shopping."

"When will you be back?"

"I don't know. I shouldn't be gone too long. If you need me, text me."

Then, looking him in the eye, she said, "And don't go anywhere."

He ordered a hamburger and french fries and, of course, a chocolate malt. At first, it felt cool to be on his own. But then he noticed that most of the others at the lunch counter were kids with their parents. He was the only one there by himself.

When he was finished eating, he swiveled around and watched children holding their parents' hands, moving from one display, one toy to the next. He longed to be a part of it. But he knew this was no longer his life.

He kept an eye on his phone for a text from his mother, but no text ever came. Finally, after two hours, she returned, with shopping bags hanging like candy canes from her arms.

She seemed to be in a hurry.

"Let's go," she said.

* * *

Now David looked down at his new shoes. They were covered with mud. So were his jeans. His mother would be mad.

But when wasn't she mad these days?

More and more, her anger seemed to be directed at David. Maybe it was because his father and brother weren't around much, making him an easy target.

All he knew is that everything he did seemed to set her off anymore. His music was too loud. His grades were too low. His clothes didn't match. His room was a mess. He didn't speak up.

His friends got in trouble for these things too. Maybe he was too sensitive, he thought. Maybe his mother didn't mean to hurt him. Maybe it was not about him at all. Maybe his mother was searching for a clearing too.

David didn't plan to follow that trail so deep into the woods that day or be so far from home. But he knew that, by leaving, he would no longer be a nuisance. He was tired of being a nuisance.

So he left. He just left.

* * *

The sun was almost down now, and the thick clouds blocked any light from the moon and the stars. David had lost the trail. In the dim light, he could make out only the silhouette of the trees all around him. The trees were like a fortress now. They made him feel safe.

But he was also cold and tired. He had walked a long way. He must be near the clearing. If only he could find it.

But then he remembered Matt said he wasn't even sure there was a clearing. Maybe he had made it up.

It reminded him of being lost in that store, more than half a lifetime ago. Except now, he knew he was on his own, and he understood how it felt to be truly alone.

He needed to rest. He stopped walking. He was surrounded by a small grove of trees. He crouched and felt along the ground for dry leaves, which he gathered into a little pile.

He lay down on the bed of leaves, pulled his hat down over his ears and eyes and stuffed his hands into the pockets of his coat. He drew his knees up to his chest and curled up as tightly as he could.

He knew there were owls and coyotes in the woods at night. But tonight everything was quiet. Everything was peaceful. For so long, all he had wanted was some peace.

He felt a gust of wind and heard the rustling of the last leaves on branches high above, leaves which, despite the change of seasons, refused to let go.

There are some leaves on some trees whose connection remains strong no matter how fierce the winter. There is something inside, unseen, which binds them.

Just as he began to fall asleep, David heard a voice in the distance. It was a woman's voice.

"David!"

Then he heard a man's voice.

"David!"

Then he heard them calling his name in unison.

It was his parents. How long it had been since he'd heard them together when they weren't fighting.

David stood up, pulled off his cap and looked in the direction of the voices. Through the darkness, he could see a clearing.

"I'm here!" he shouted.

Who is Peter Caruso?

His alarm went off, as usual, at 5:00 a.m. Five minutes earlier, his Bodum Bistro coffeemaker clicked on and began brewing two cups of aged Sumatran coffee. By the time he went to the bathroom and got to the kitchen, the air was heavy with the aroma of burnt spice.

He poured the first cup into a black ceramic mug. The thermal carafe would keep the second cup hot until he was ready for it, after he worked out, in 90 minutes. He would sip it on his way to work.

Now, though, he made his way back down the hallway to his study. The room was dark. He reached inside the doorway and felt along the rough, brick wall until his fingertips bumped into a wooden switch plate. He flipped the switch, and a lamp on his desk filled the room with pale yellow light. He stepped across the plush oriental rug. It was soft and warm on his bare feet. He sat down in the high-back leather chair and logged on to his computer.

Then as he did every morning, he Googled his name, Peter Caruso. As he waited for the search results, he picked up a pencil on his desk and began doodling on a scratch pad. *Who is Peter Caruso?* he scribbled.

Three news stories popped up, two analyst reports and one blog. They'd all been posted overnight. He sipped his coffee and leaned in for a closer look.

It was all the result of a presentation he had made at an investor conference the day before. There he had challenged his fellow investment advisers to "double down" on value investing by "buying far more cheap stocks, then not hesitating to unload them."

To support his case, he announced that, by following this strategy, many of his clients were now seeing a 20% return on their investments, more than twice the market average, after only two years.

During the Q&A session, he got plenty of push back, just as he expected. His lively back-and-forth with several investors and his refusal to divulge his "proprietary formulas" for determining the best "cheap stocks" and when to sell made for colorful quotes and good copy.

He knew how to make news. His firm, Taft and Irving, knew that too. Whenever they needed good PR, they turned to Peter.

He delivered superbly, making a name for himself in the process. In financial circles, he had become a celebrity. Analysts, investors, journalists all wanted to talk with Peter Caruso.

This star quality and his ability to use it to bring in big-money clients made Peter one of Taft and Irving's most valuable assets. No wonder he made partner at 32. No wonder he was now rumored to be a CEO contender.

He smiled, sat back in his chair and closed his eyes. He held his coffee mug in both hands, just under his chin, and breathed in the sweet, earthy aroma. The steam warmed the inside of his nose.

Then he opened his eyes and looked across the room at a large, cherry bookcase. It held dozens of books and an array of exotic objects he had collected from around the world: a white jade Buddha, a glazed ceramic vase, an intricately carved sandstone horse.

But his eyes focused on a single piece, set back in the center of the bookcase, that was far less refined: a watercolor painting of a small, red-brick house. It was the house where he grew up. He had made that picture when he was six years old.

He remembered sitting in his front yard and sketching it, then going to his room and painting it with watercolors. He remembered how proud and excited he felt when his mother framed it and hung it on his bedroom wall.

It was the only piece in his apartment from his childhood, the only hint of a middle-class world on the twelfth floor of a luxury high-rise on the Upper West Side of Manhattan, the only inexpensive thing in the place.

His eyes were focused on it now because he liked to be reminded of what it felt like to create something. He was no longer creating. Now his days were spent optimizing assets. That's what his life was about.

But his little painting was a reminder that wasn't always the case and long before he was collecting art, he was creating it.

Looking at it made him feel half-empty. It was a feeling he was having more and more, a feeling he could not seem to shake.

* * *

He walked to the door and was about to turn off the light. But he stopped and looked at the solid brick wall in front of him. It was so plain. This morning there was something about it that made him pause. He reached out and ran his fingertips over it, then pressed the palm of his hand against it.

He closed his eyes and thought of the summer when he was 15, the summer he had worked with his father. His father was a bricklayer. It was just the two of them.

That was more than 25 years ago, and he no longer remembered the details. But he remembered the feeling of creating something real — a wall, a patio, a walkway — of working with something he could hold in his hands.

He never worked so hard. Every day, his whole body ached. Before that summer, he had pretty much decided he would go to college. By the end, any doubt was removed. He realized he could never work with his hands for a living. Maybe that was his father's intention.

Now, though, as he touched the rough surface of the wall, he realized how much he missed it. Not laying brick. But creating something real.

* * *

He stepped out of the shower, dried off and stepped onto his Fitbit scale. 157.8 pounds. *Good. Still under 160.*

It was Friday. Some in his office had begun to dress casually on Fridays. But he would be seeing clients, and he always dressed to impress. He picked out a dark blue Armani suit, a light blue Ferragamo tie and, as always, a freshly pressed, white cotton shirt.

He got dressed, then checked himself out in a floor-length mirror in his bedroom. The dark suit and light tie were an elegant combination. How could his clients not be impressed?

Back in his kitchen, he poured a bottle of water, a scoop of whey protein powder and a cup of frozen berries into his Vitamix blender, pressed the button for smoothie, poured it into a tall glass and drank it down.

Then he poured his second cup of coffee into a small, stainless steel travel mug, grabbed his iPhone and Maui Jims, locked his apartment door behind him and pressed the button for the elevator.

When he got to the lobby, the receptionist and door man, Robert, greeted him.

"Good morning, Mr. Caruso."

"Good morning, Robert."

"You're looking very sharp this morning."

"Well, thank you, Robert. I'm meeting with some high rollers today."

"How can they resist?"

Peter smiled.

"That's what I'm banking on, Robert."

"My money's on you, Mr. Caruso," Robert said, as he opened the door for him.

The sun was just rising, and he put on his sunglasses. Robert hurried by him and opened the right rear door of a black Lincoln Town Car that was waiting at the curb.

"Thank you, Robert."

Peter pulled a tightly folded $100 bill from his right pants pocket.

"Have a great weekend," he said, discretely handing Robert the bill. Neither of the men looked down at the money changing hands. But Peter looked around to see who might be watching. Sometimes if someone was walking by, he would unfold the bill just a little and pause for a moment before handing it off.

"Give my best to Barbara."

"Thank you, Mr. Caruso. You have a wonderful weekend."

* * *

The fall air was crisp, but it was not yet cool enough for an overcoat. It was his favorite time of the year. He especially liked driving past Central Park when the leaves were turning. It reminded him of home.

"Good morning, Mr. Caruso," said his driver.

"Good morning, Charles."

"Beautiful morning. Would you like to drive through the park today?"

"That's very tempting, Charles. But I think I'll pass this morning. I'll be running there tomorrow, and I need to get ready for a meeting. But thanks."

"Very good," Charles said, taking the hint and giving it a little gas as he headed south toward Midtown.

Tomorrow would be fun. After running in the park in the morning, he would take in the new Matisse exhibition at the Museum of Modern Art. In the evening, he would get together at a dinner party with friends.

He bought a new Cesare Attolini cashmere blazer and Bruno Magli shoes just for the occasion. Trendy clothes had become his signature at these parties. And good wine. Tomorrow he would bring a bottle of Sassicaia from Tuscany, a 2006 he'd been saving.

Now he arrived at his office building. Charles got out, scurried around the front of the car and opened the door.

"Have a great day, Mr. Caruso."

"Thank you, Charles. I'll see you back here a little before noon."

* * *

Ariana, Taft and Irving's pretty and perennially upbeat receptionist, greeted him as he got off the elevator on the sixteenth floor.

"Good morning, Mr. Caruso," she said cheerfully, looking up from her computer. "And congratulations on all the good PR this morning!"

"Good morning, Ariana. Yes, I saw that. Do you really think it's okay?"

"Oh, yes. And the photos of you. Very fine."

"Thank you, Ariana," he said, smiling. "You've just made my day."

As he made his way to his office in the corner, several other colleagues congratulated him too. He acted modest. But inside, he was beaming.

"Good morning, Mr. Caruso," said his secretary, Pam. She was sitting in her cubicle, just outside his office.

"Good morning, Pam."

"You're looking very elegant today."

"Well, thank you. It's a big day, you know."

He had only three appointments but all with heavy hitters: one in the morning, one over lunch and one in the afternoon.

Their portfolios were quite different, and his proposals were carefully tailored. But his aim for all three was the same: to convince them to invest more. If they bought what he was selling, he figured it would net him an extra hundred grand. Not a bad day.

"I've inserted a set of all the latest articles mentioning you in the front pocket of each of your binders," Pam said.

Three binders, each of them sporting the Taft and Irving logo, lay in a perfect row across a walnut credenza that ran along his window, perpendicular to his large, ebony desk. Next to each binder was a slender file on that client. He liked to have all his materials for the day lined up there in the morning.

"Thank you, Pam. You're always a step ahead."

* * *

His first meeting could not have gone better. Now he was sitting at a table at Bellini, his second client's favorite restaurant. They had just ordered and were sipping bourbon.

Peter was just about to wrap up the small talk and begin his pitch when his phone began vibrating. Who on earth would be calling him now? During lunch, his business calls were automatically routed to Pam.

"Excuse me," he said, sliding his phone out of his jacket pocket and looking embarrassed.

"Of course."

He looked down at the caller's name. It was Maria, his sister.

"Hello?"

"Pete, it's Maria."

She sounded upset.

"Maria, what's up?"

"It's Dad."

"Dad?"

"He had another heart attack."

"Is he okay?"

"We're not sure."

"What do you mean?"

"He's in surgery."

"Where's Mom?"

"She's here with me, waiting at the hospital."

"Do you think I should come home?"

Silence.

"Maria, do you think I should come home?"

"Yes. Yes, Pete, I do."

"I'll leave as soon as I can."

"Okay."

"Tell Dad I'm on my way."

"Okay. I'll tell him."

* * *

"Nice suit."

Peter blinked. He had been staring out the window as the plane took off. Now he looked down and realized he was still wearing his suit.

"Thank you," he said to the man sitting next to him.

He had stopped by his apartment just long enough to pack a few things before heading to LaGuardia. He had been in such a rush that he forgot to change clothes.

Charles, who had been waiting at the restaurant, took him directly to his apartment. Peter called Pam on the way to fill her in and ask her to book him on the next flight to St. Louis.

After a quick stop at his apartment, Charles drove him directly to the airport. Uncharacteristically, Peter was silent the whole way. When they arrived, he let himself out as Charles grabbed his carry-on bag from the trunk.

"Good luck, Mr. Caruso. My prayers are with you."

"Thank you, Charles."

He handed him a $100 bill. No one was watching. He didn't care.

* * *

Now he turned back to the window, looked down at the ships along the Hudson and began thinking about his father.

His name was Dominic. He had come to the United States from Italy with his parents, Angelo and Rose, when he was eight.

Angelo was a bricklayer. No one in his family had ever left Italy. But the war had left his poor town even poorer, and he wanted a better life for Rose and Dominic, their only child. And so Angelo made the biggest and toughest decision of his life: to leave his homeland for the US.

He'd heard from friends there were many Italians living in a place called St. Louis. People were building a lot of houses there. And so in 1950, he sold everything he owned and struck out for St. Louis.

The three of them took a boat across the Mediterranean to Portugal and then a ship across the Atlantic to Ellis Island. From there, they took a ferry to Jersey City and, from there, trains to St. Louis. In all, the journey took them nearly three weeks.

When they arrived in St. Louis, a man at the train station, himself an Italian immigrant, heard them talking. He asked where they were heading. Angelo told him they were looking for a place to stay in "little Italy." He suggested they go see a priest named Father Capella at St. Ambrose Church in a section of town called The Hill.

Father Capella knew everyone there. He found Angelo and his family a place to stay right away. Not only that, he knew of a home-builder, one of his parishioners, who was looking for bricklayers. Angelo went to the construction site the next morning and was hired on the spot.

The crew chief was impressed with Angelo from day one. He didn't know English. But he needed only glance at a blueprint to understand a project, and he had an intuitive sense for the flow of the work. He was strong and fast and took few breaks.

Bricklaying was in his blood. His father and grandfather had also been bricklayers, and he hoped his own son would carry on the family tradition. And so when Dominic was only nine, Angelo began taking him to work on Saturdays.

Rose was not happy about this, but she had seen it coming. When Dominic was a toddler, Angelo would lie on the floor with him and show him how create little buildings with wooden blocks. By four, Dominic was designing his own little buildings. By five, he was creating little villages, sometimes sprawling from room to room in their small house. Rose grumbled about the mess. Angelo bought Dominic more blocks.

He took his son to work with him for the first time when he was eight. Dominic told Rose he would just let the boy watch. But after watching his father butter the edges of a brick with wet cement, Dominic picked up a trowel and joined him.

Angelo didn't say much. He didn't have to. The boy learned just by watching. And he worked alongside his father all day, laying one brick for every two of his father's, but just as straight.

Dominic was a natural. By 10, he had learned all the basics of bricklaying. By 12, he was sketching interesting new designs for walkways and patios. They were so good that Angelo shared them with his crew chief. He liked them so much that he began using them as a selling point with customers. By 14, Dominic was as strong as his father. By 15, he could handle small projects on his own. Angelo was thrilled.

In the 1950s, homebuilding was booming in St. Louis. Builders vied for the best workers. Angelo always had work, and he earned more in a day than he would have in a month back home.

The family had been renting a place, but soon they had enough money to buy their own house. It was a small place, next to a bakery on The Hill. But it was theirs. There was even enough money for Angelo to buy a used Chevy. He had never owned a car.

All three Carusos began to learn English. But Dominic picked it up much faster because only English was spoken in school at St. Ambrose. He fit in well there. Many of the other students were also the children of Italian immigrants. They all lived on The Hill. The whole neighborhood had the feel of a big Italian family.

Life was good for the Carusos until Dominic was 17. Coming home from school one afternoon, he saw his father's car parked on the street. It was at least two hours before his father ever got home from work.

He went inside and heard a strange voice coming from his parents' bedroom. The door was open, and he looked in. It was Doctor DeToma. He was examining his mother, who was sitting up in bed. His father was sitting on a chair next to the bed. His mother's blouse was undone and, seeing Dominic, she quickly covered herself.

His father got up and motioned to Dominic to come with him. He followed him into the kitchen.

"What's going on, Dad?"

"Your mother is ill. The doctor says it is serious. He thinks it might be cancer."

His mother had always been frail, and lately she had not been feeling well. But cancer? It had never entered their minds.

But it ravaged her, and less than three months later, the day after Dominic's eighteenth birthday, it took her life.

Rose was Angelo's anchor. Without her, he felt adrift. He was not a man given to introspection, but his world was rocked, and he began to reflect deeply on his situation.

He realized that this place was not really his home, especially without Rose. His home was in Italy, the place he had known all his life, near the sea, among family and friends who spoke a language he did not labor to understand.

But he also realized that, for his son, this place was indeed home. He knew Dominic would be successful here and carry on the family tradition. But he also knew that, as his son became a man, he himself would grow old, and he did not want to saddle his son with caring for an old man.

Moving to the US was the toughest decision Angelo had ever made. Now he made one even tougher: to return to Italy. Fighting back tears, he told Dominic the day after he graduated from high school. Overwhelmed, Dominic said he would go too.

"No," his father said. "I want you to stay. You'll make a better life for yourself here."

A few days later, Angelo signed over the titles for his house and his car to his son. Then Dominic drove him to the train station and kissed him goodbye.

He would never see his father again.

* * *

"Sir, would you like something to drink?"

The flight attendant startled him.

"Yes, coffee, please. Black."

Sipping his coffee, Peter turned back to the window.

He thought again about that summer when he had worked with his father. He remembered the first day on the job and how odd it seemed to see him in work clothes. He usually left the house before Peter woke up. After work, he came in through the back door and went directly to his bathroom to take a shower. By the time Peter saw his father most evenings for dinner, he had changed into dress clothes. That's how he dressed on the weekends too. On Sundays, he even wore a tie.

And it made him wonder: why was his father always so dressed up at home? So at work one day, he asked him.

"You see me now, Peter, as I usually am. But no one else does. They see the man I want them to see. That's the Dominic Caruso the world knows."

His father's answer puzzled him. And it begged the question: Why? Why did he want people to see him this way?

He didn't press his father that day. But over the course of the summer, he asked him many questions, and he learned much.

He learned, for example, that when his father and grandfather were working on larger crews, the loud, rough men who framed the houses they bricked would call them "guineas." There was a pecking order in construction, and many of the workers looked down on bricklayers. Only Italians would do such menial work, they said.

His grandfather didn't seem very bothered by it, maybe because his English was not good. But it upset his father greatly.

It wasn't so much the name calling, but rather the idea that his work — and he, by extension — was somehow less. At first, it made him angry. Then it made him wonder if he really did measure up.

At that point, as much as he loved his work, given the option, he would have gladly done something else. Many of his friends were going off to college. He wished he could join them. He wished he could do something respectable in the eyes of the world. But bricklaying was the only thing he knew. Now that he was alone, it was the only way he could make a living.

He could not change this. But he could change himself. He could change what people thought of him.

He began taking jobs he could do alone, so that few would ever see him at work in the first place. When he wasn't working, he began wearing nice clothes. He sold his father's old Chevy and bought a new Buick. He began spending less time on The Hill and more time meeting new people, including young professionals. He sold his house on The Hill and got an apartment downtown.

Except for his work, he changed everything and became a new man.

* * *

Dominic was handsome, refined and spoke with a slight accent, which women found charming. One weekend at a party, he met a beautiful young school teacher named Marisa. They were each sipping a glass of red wine. By the time their glasses were empty, they had fallen in love.

That evening, Marisa asked Dominic what he did for a living. When he told her, she was surprised but not deterred. If anything, it made him even more intriguing.

But he was quick to insist that Marisa not talk about what he did for a living. He told her that, if anyone asked, she should simply say he "worked in design." She found this curious, but it was a half-truth she could live with.

In a year, they were married. They bought a small house in a suburb of St. Louis. Even with two incomes, though, they could hardly afford the place. But no one knew because they carried themselves with such grace.

To everyone Peter knew growing up, his father was a simply a dashing, dapper, quiet man who always drove a new Buick.

"You become who people think you are, Peter," his father told him that summer. "You become whoever you want to be."

* * *

"What do you want to do, Peter?" asked Mrs. Henry, his high school guidance counselor.

"I want to be a stock broker and live in New York."

"That's pretty specific," she said, smiling. "Why?"

"I want to make a lot of money."

"Do you know anything about becoming a stockbroker?"

"I know I need to go to college."

"That's right. You'll need to major in business, probably finance. And you should think about an MBA too."

"Sounds good. What are my options?"

His confidence made her smile. She swiveled in her chair, slid open the top drawer of a metal file cabinet and picked out half a dozen brochures.

"Here are a few ideas to get you started. These are all good business schools. There are a few in the Midwest and few out East. The ones out East are a little pricey. You might want to start with the ones closer to home."

"Thank you," he said, grabbing the brochures and heading for the door.

"Peter."

"Yes?"

"Remember us when you get rich."

"I will."

He went to his room after dinner that evening and read every brochure cover to cover. All the schools looked good.

But he knew which one he wanted right away: NYU. It had a business school, and it was in the heart of Manhattan, the center of the business world. Tuition was steep. But he figured with his father's modest income, he'd qualify for lots of aid, and with his good grades, he could get a scholarship.

And that's just what happened.

He earned his undergraduate degree in three years, then his MBA in a year, graduating with honors. During the summers, he interned with several investment firms in Manhattan. Even before he finished his MBA, Peter got offers from several top financial firms.

They were all impressive. But Taft and Irving offered the best starting salary and a signing bonus. Plus he liked the way they called him "Mr. Caruso."

That was 20 years ago. He had indeed become a stock broker, made lots of money and was living in New York.

"You become whoever you want to be," his dad had told him. And so he had.

But he still couldn't shake the feeling of being half-empty.

* * *

He called Maria as soon as his plane touched down.

"How's Dad?"

"Stable."

"Is he going to be okay?"

"We think so. They put in three stents. Oh, Pete. Dad had something the doctor called 'the widow-maker.' It was a close call."

"How's he feeling?"

"Pretty good. He's sitting up in bed. He's a strong man, Pete."

"How's Mom?"

"She's okay."

"Good. We should be at the gate in a few minutes. I'll come straight to the hospital. Tell Mom and Dad I'll be there in about 45 minutes."

"Okay, Pete. Room 405. See you soon."

* * *

It was early evening when he landed, but the sun had not yet set. He hadn't been home in nearly two years, and he was grateful for the chance to take in the landscape on the taxi ride before nightfall.

He had missed the low hills, the broad valleys, the rolling prairie. He remembered riding his bike along the back roads near his home as a boy and stopping in different places and pulling out his drawing book and sitting down to sketch a tree or a field or a stream.

Sketching those things filled him up. There was something about looking at a sunset or horses in a pasture or snow on a grove of pine trees and then expressing those things in his own way that made him happy.

He made hundreds of pictures: nature scenes, abstract designs, houses, barns, horses, cars and people, including portraits of his parents and his sister. He signed them all "Peter." He and his mother, his biggest fan, picked their favorites. She framed them and hung them on his bedroom walls.

But when Peter turned 12, his thoughts began to shift from the act of creating to the idea of painting *for a living*. Could he do it? Would he be good enough? Should he not strive for more? Would he make any money? What would people think of him?

No one had ever told him to become an artist. It just came naturally. But now, for the first time, he had doubts. He began drawing and painting less until, for reasons he no longer remembered and maybe never fully understood, Peter put his pencils and paints away.

* * *

He found room 405, took a deep breath and peeked inside. His father was sitting up in bed, eating dinner. His mother and sister were sitting in chairs on either side of the bed.

"Oh!" the women cried.

They both rushed to him. He wrapped his arms around them, held them close and kissed their cheeks.

"Peter, I'm so glad you're here," said his mother.

She looked tired and so much older.

"We saw you on TV last week, Pete," said Maria. "You looked so good."

"But even more handsome in person," said his mother, pinching his cheek.

"Peter," said his father. "Thank you for coming."

Peter walked over and shook his father's hand. It was large, thick and calloused.

"It's good to see you, Dad. How are you?"

"Well, the doctor said I made it here just in time. And Father Earl said God doesn't need any more bricklayers in heaven today."

"I'm glad you're okay," Peter said.

"So I guess I need to have a heart attack for you to come visit your mother."

"No, Dad. I'm sorry. I'll visit more often."

"We'd love that, Peter," his mother said.

"We sure would," said Maria.

"How about this Christmas?" his mother said, seizing the moment.

How could he say no?

"Yes, Mom. I'll come home this Christmas."

"Oh, Peter. That would be wonderful."

"The kids will be so glad to see you again," said Maria.

A nurse knocked and stepped into the room.

"May I take your tray, Mr. Caruso?"

"Absolutely," he said, pushing back his half-eaten dinner. "My compliments to the chef."

"Now, Dom," Peter's mother said.

"Sorry," he said, grinning at Peter.

"You know," said his mother, "Maria and I were just talking about going down the cafeteria to get something to eat. Maybe this would be a good time for you two to catch up a bit."

"Maybe Peter's hungry too," his father said.

"No, I'm fine, Dad."

"Can we bring you something?"

"No, thanks."

"Okay," said his mother. "We'll be back soon. You boys be on your best behavior."

"We'll try, Mom. Enjoy your dinner."

His mother leaned down and gently kissed her husband on the lips.

"I love you, Dom."

"And I love you."

When the women had left, Peter pulled a chair over to the bed and sat down.

"Peter, there's something I need to tell you."

"What's that, Dad?"

"I was wrong."

"You were wrong?"

"Yes."

"About what?"

"I gave you some very bad advice. When we worked together that summer, I told you that you become who people think you are. But I was wrong."

"What do you mean?"

"You *are* who you *are*. What people think doesn't matter. The most important thing is to be yourself."

"I don't think you gave me bad advice, Dad."

"Yes, I did," he said, looking away. "And I set a bad example for you too. I'm a bricklayer. But I wanted people to think I was something else, something more. I've lived my life as an imposter. I regret that."

"Dad, I think you're being too hard on yourself."

"This is not just about me, Peter," looking his son in the eye. "It's about you too."

"About me?"

"Do you remember what you wanted to be when you were a boy?"

"Yeah. I wanted to be an artist."

"That's right. And do you remember what I told you about that?"

"No."

"I told you not to pursue it because there's no money in it. Become a stockbroker, I said. Move to New York. Those were my ideas, Peter, not yours. You were impressionable, and I put those ideas in your head. It's the worst thing I've ever done."

"It's okay, Dad. I turned out okay, didn't I?"

His father looked at him and sighed.

"You're rich and successful, Peter. But are you happy?"

He looked down and didn't answer.

"We must be who we really are. It's the only way to be happy."

"Dad ..."

"I am a bricklayer, Peter. That's all I've ever been. And now I know that's enough."

Peter didn't know what to say.

"Find out who you are, Peter. It's not too late. And it will be enough."

He looked up at his father. His eyes were filled with tears. He had never seen his father cry.

"I'm sorry, Peter."

"It's okay, Dad."

He got up and held his father's hand, then bent down and kissed him on the forehead.

"It's okay. All is forgiven."

* * *

He drove his mother home in his father's Buick.

"You look good, but a little thin, Peter. Are you sure you're eating well?"

"I'm eating great, Mom."

"What did you have for dinner tonight?"

"Okay. I'll pick something up on the way."

"Don't be silly. I'll fix you some pasta when we get home."

"Mom, how are you doing?"

"I'm okay, thanks. Your father gave us quite a scare this morning. But he's going to be okay, and so I'm fine."

"You look tired, Mom. How's your health?"

"I'm fine, Peter. I'm just getting old. But I'm fine. Really."

"Good. Mom, Dad told me something back at the hospital I'd never heard before."

"Oh?"

"Yeah, he said he talked me out of becoming an artist when I was a kid. Is that true?"

His mother stiffened in her seat and looked straight ahead. She didn't answer.

"Mom, is it true?"

"Yes, it's true," she said quietly.

She started to cry.

"I'm sorry, Mom. I didn't mean to upset you."

"It's okay, Peter," she said, wiping her eyes. "Your father just wanted the best for you. He wanted you to have the type of life he could only dream of."

"And how did you feel about that?"

"About what?"

"About me not becoming an artist?"

"It broke my heart."

"What?"

"It made me sad to see you stop painting. I should have put my foot down. I hoped you would paint again one day. And then when you did so well in school and business, I started to think that your father was right."

"Do you really think he was right, Mom?"

"I'm proud of everything you've done, Peter."

"But do you think I missed my true calling?"

She didn't answer.

"Mom, you don't have to —"

"That's yours, Peter, something only you can know."

* * *

He parked in his parents' driveway. They had a garage. But he knew that, unless it was snowing, his father liked to park outside.

His mother unlocked the front door, and he followed her inside. The decor was spare, as it had always been. His parents had created a Feng shui look long before it was fashionable because it allowed them to buy less stuff.

"Make yourself at home, dear. You can sleep in your old room. Why don't you go change while I get supper ready?"

"Thanks, Mom. It's good to be home."

The house was small, a three-bedroom ranch, with no basement or upstairs. Peter's old bedroom was smaller than the kitchen in his apartment in New York.

He flipped on the light and looked around the room. Everything was just as it was when he was growing up.

On the walls, there must have been 30 paintings and drawings, each of them framed and signed "Peter." He had created all of them by the time he was 12.

His old desk stood next to his bed. On it, in a frame, was a photograph of him in kindergarten, his first school picture. It was pasted on white paper, on which was printed "I am Peter Caruso" in crayon.

He pulled out the small wooden desk chair, sat down and picked up the frame.

"I am Peter Caruso," he said to himself.

Then he wondered aloud: "Who is Peter Caruso?"

He got up and changed into jeans and a sweatshirt. Then he sat down on his bed, grabbed his cell phone and dialed his boss' number, knowing he would no longer be in the office.

"Bill, it's Peter. I'm in St. Louis. My dad is going to be okay. But there are some things here that need my attention. I'm going to take a week. I'll call Pam and rearrange my schedule. Thanks for understanding. I'll see you in a week."

He got up, sat back down in his desk chair and pulled out the drawer. There was his old watercolor set in a white plastic case. He snapped open the lid, revealing a row of eight oval cakes. The paint was dried and cracked, but the colors were still vibrant.

He plucked his old red paint brush out of a groove in the plastic and twisted the bristles between his fingertips. They were stiff. But he pushed them into the palm of his hand, and they gave way and became soft again, like new.

Show Me

It was four in the morning, but Mother didn't have to work hard to wake me. As soon as she whispered my name, I knew what day it was. It was the day Daddy would take my younger brother and me fishing, a once-a-summer adventure.

We jumped out of bed and got dressed in the dark. When we got to the dining room, Mother had breakfast waiting. As we ate, she packed our lunches in the kitchen and filled Daddy's tall, red plaid Thermos with hot coffee.

Daddy appeared, clean-shaven and smelling like Mennen Skin Bracer.

"Ready?" he said.

Daddy was a man of action.

He had stowed our fishing gear in the trunk of our Dodge Dart the night before. We tossed in our sack lunches, and Daddy carefully laid in his Thermos. Mother kissed us all goodbye, and we were off.

We drove through the darkness. At last we arrived at Springdale Lake. It was a pay lake, so we went directly to a small white building to pay the fee and buy worms.

An older lady was the only one there. She was sitting in a chair when we came in. A metal shoe horn clanged against the glass door as we opened it, and the noise woke her up. I suppose we were her first customers.

After we settled up, we set out to find a good fishing spot. The lake was large, and we walked around the bank for a long time until Daddy found a place he liked.

My brother and I had bamboo poles. Daddy had a rod and reel that looked like it had been designed by NASA engineers. We watched in awe as he set our lines.

Before we could get our lines in the water, though, we encountered a problem. Daddy was putting his wallet and loose change in his tackle box. I guess he didn't want to risk losing his money while we were fishing. He looked at the receipt from his transaction that morning and realized the woman had given him too much change.

"We have to go back," he said.

So we left our gear and followed Daddy back around the lake to the small white building. It was still dark.

The woman seemed surprised to see us again. Daddy explained she'd given him too much change. She said it was okay, but Daddy insisted on making it right.

We then walked all the way back around the lake, watched the sun rise and fished the whole glorious day.

* * *

Early this year, my father lay dying in a hospice facility. We were relieved he could spend his last days in such a place because my siblings and I could be with him. For much of the last year of his life, Daddy lived alone, quarantined in his retirement community because of the pandemic.

Now, though, my brother and I sat at the sides of his bed, holding his hands. Daddy could no longer see or speak, but he could still hear. I recounted the story about fishing at Springdale Lake and told him everything I ever learned about integrity I learned from watching him that day. Daddy smiled and squeezed our hands.

My father was a man of few words. In fact, I don't remember much of what he said to me. But I remember everything he did around me, and what he did inspired and shaped me.

Some people tell us what to do. Others show us.

Sorrow

They All Run Together

"Did you hear the news?"

"What news?"

"About the mass shooting."

"Where?"

"Hmm, let me think."

"You mean in Indianapolis?"

"No, the one last night."

"In Texas?"

"No, that was last week."

"You're not thinking of the one in Wisconsin, are you?"

"Wisconsin? No, that was a while ago."

"Well, I'm not sure then."

"Me either. Sorry I mentioned it."

“No worries. It’s hard to keep them all straight.”

“I know. They all run together.”

“Isn’t that sad?”

“Yeah.”

Watercolors

"I'm sorry," the doctor said to the young couple sitting in the corner of the hospital room. "Sarah is gone. We did everything we could."

Karen put her head in her hands and let out an awful moan. David wrapped his arms around her. He looked up at the doctor and nodded, as if to dismiss him. Saying nothing more, the doctor slipped out.

The two of them sat there, holding one another and crying for a long time before David got up and asked the nurse if they could see their daughter again.

* * *

As a girl, Karen loved to paint with watercolors. Her mother gave her a set of watercolor paints for her fourth birthday. Karen loved dipping her brush in a cup of water, wiping it across the little cakes of vibrant colors and creating images on sheets of white paper.

At first, her work was wild, a flurry of bold and colorful brushstrokes. But before long, recognizable objects began to emerge: a tree, a house, the sun.

By six, Karen was painting basic landscapes. By seven, she was painting the sea. She had never been to the ocean. But her parents had a coffee table book which featured a spectacular collection of photographs of the natural world. Karen used to study the pictures in that book for hours.

One day, she brought the book into her bedroom, where she now painted with an easel. She opened it wide to a favorite photo: a two-page, panoramic shot of the Atlantic Ocean taken from the docks of a fishing town in New England. She propped the book up on her desk next to her easel.

She painted that scene over and over, improving it each time. She even began blending colors to get just the right shades for a wooden boat, a swooping seagull and the glint of noonday sun on the waves.

Recognizing her talent and her promise, Karen's parents enrolled her in art school at age eight. Karen blossomed, painting all kinds of things.

She was mesmerized by things. She could sit and gaze at the horizon or a hillside of wildflowers for hours. To Karen, such things seemed like natural objects of art.

She learned to use acrylics, pastels and oil paints, but she always came back to watercolors.

"They just feel right," she said.

When Karen was 14, several of her paintings were featured in a local art exhibition. Afterwards, a woman contacted her mother to ask if she could buy one. Her mother had Karen follow up with the woman directly. She sold her first painting for $50. The young artist was ecstatic.

Karen kept painting all through high school, and her paintings began to be featured in regional art shows. The broader exposure led to even more interest in her work, and she began selling most of the paintings she exhibited.

Some people asked Karen to do portraits, but she demurred. "People move too much," she said.

Buoyed by the prospect of a steady income from painting, Karen decided not to go to college but instead open her own art gallery. It was there, during an open house one Friday evening, she met David.

They fell in love and were married a year later. Two years after that, Sarah was born. She lived just three days.

* * *

After Sarah died, Karen felt lost. She tried to paint but couldn't. Nothing seemed to interest her anymore, not even painting.

One day, she went to a nearby park. She had long loved immersing herself in nature there. Sometimes she even brought her easel and paints to try to record the beauty of the trees, ponds and meadowed hills.

Now, though, as she walked a familiar trail through the woods, Karen seemed oblivious to her surroundings.

At the end of the trail she came upon a large jungle gym. About a dozen children were playing on it as their mothers kept watch.

At first, the children made Karen think of Sarah, and she was tempted to keep walking. But she was tired and sat down on a bench to rest.

She watched the children at play. She saw the joy in their faces.

Then she closed her eyes. In her mind, she could see Sarah's face. She was smiling.

Karen opened her eyes and looked at the scene anew. In days past, her eyes would have been drawn to the trees all around her. Now the trees seem to fade into the background and bring the happy children into sharp relief. These children were now Karen's focus. They were now her center point.

Karen drove home. She found a photograph David had taken of Sarah as a newborn. Her eyes were open, and she had a faint smile on her face. Karen remembered her daughter looking up at her at that very moment. It was a moment of great happiness.

She went into their second bedroom, which served as her art studio at home. She clipped the photograph to her easel and began recreating the face of her daughter.

* * *

After that, Karen began painting again. She painted every day. But she no longer painted things. Now she painted people.

Karen's paintings became more popular than ever. People said they could see a certain joy in the faces of the people in Karen's paintings. They said her paintings brought them comfort.

Now Karen painted only with watercolors. With every face, she thought of Sarah. Sometimes this made her cry, and her tears would blend with her paint.

Regret

He gets up early every morning. He makes himself a cup of coffee and sits longways on the sofa in his family room alongside two large windows in the back of his house.

It's always dark when he gets up. In the winter, he used to watch the sky lighten and a line of trees in the nearby woods emerge, all hardwoods except for one big evergreen.

There was something about that evergreen that bothered him. It seemed out of place. It just didn't fit.

One day, he went into the woods with a chainsaw. He made his way to the evergreen, a stout, 40-foot Norway spruce, and cut it down at the base. It was far too big to drag away, so he sliced off the branches and cut the trunk into pieces, which he carried home for firewood.

These days, he sits on the other end of his sofa in the morning. He doesn't want to face the hardwood trees, which now look monotonous and lonely, like stalwart soldiers standing at perpetual attention in honor of a fallen comrade. The very sight of them fills him with regret.

Perfect

Maddie was the prettiest baby her family and parents' friends had ever seen. Even strangers stopped and stared. With blond hair, big blue eyes and rosy cheeks, she looked like she belonged on the label of a baby food jar.

Her mother had lots of baby pictures taken at a local studio. The studio featured its photos of Maddie on its website. Her mother sent the link to all her friends.

Maddie grew up beautifully, the most popular girl in her class. But when she hit puberty, her looks began to change. She gained weight, and her slender face grew round. Her blond hair turned brown. She needed braces and glasses.

Some of her classmates began to make fun of her, but Maddie didn't mind. She liked the way she looked.

Her mother, though, was disturbed by Maddie's changing appearance.

"Don't worry," she said. "I can help you."

"But I don't need help, Mom."

"You'll thank me later," her mother said.

She signed Maddie up with a modeling agency.

"I want you to turn her back into model material," she told the lady there.

They put Maddie on a strict diet and rigorous exercise program. They swapped her glasses for contacts and her metal braces for clear plastic aligners. They bleached her teeth, waxed her face and dyed her hair.

Her mother was thrilled by the transformation.

"You'll be a famous model after all," she said.

At her first photo shoot under contract, the photographer made Maddie strike a variety of most unnatural poses. She felt uncomfortable, but she obliged and managed to smile, even though she felt like crying.

"Perfect," the photographer said.

Wild Child

Justin was a wild child. That's what people called him anyway. Free spirit. Did what he wanted. Talked back. Skipped school. Ran around barefoot in thunderstorms. Gave his parents fits.

"Behave," his mother pleaded.

"Go to your room," his father demanded.

But Justin wouldn't change. In desperation, his mother took him to a doctor, who prescribed medicine, which settled him. Helped him study, get good grades. No more back talk. No more running around in the rain. Straight As. Scholarship. College. Job. Wife. Kids.

"Liam's a wild child," Justin's wife said.

"Let him be," said Justin, watching the dark clouds move in.

Spring

Through the slightly opened window, he could smell the sweet fragrance of lilacs and dogwood blossoms borne on the warm air from the courtyard below.

At least they allowed him this one connection with the outside world. He guessed they figured that a bedridden old man isn't going to escape, especially from two floors up.

He loved spring. It reminded him of playing baseball as a boy in an empty lot down the street from his house. He loved the feel of the soggy earth beneath his feet. He loved the freedom of shedding his winter coat.

Freedom. It had been so long since he knew what it was like to come and go as he pleased. Now his days were spent in this hospital bed. They served his meals here. They gave him pills to swallow here. They changed his diaper here.

He gazed through the window at the setting sun. Soon it would be dark. There would be one more check tonight, then lights out.

He waited until his nurse was gone. She had left his window open just a crack. Maybe she knew how he felt about spring. Had he told her? He couldn't remember.

He pulled back his blanket and sheets and swung his legs over the side of his bed. His feet dangled well above the floor. He slipped off the bed and came down hard on the bare soles of his feet. A pain shot through his legs, but he resisted calling out. He hoped no one had heard the thud.

He shuffled over to a chair in the corner and sat down, looking around his room from a new vantage point. This was where his visitors sat. No one had visited in quite a while.

He looked at his bed. These days, it seemed more like a prison. How strange it seemed to not be lying there now and to see it empty, like a prisoner surveying his vacant cell from the outside. For a moment, he felt like a man again.

The window was now less than two feet away. He could feel the warm breeze on his face. It called to him like springtime beckons a child to come out and play.

He knew what he had to do. He stood and slowly made his way back to his bed. He peeled back the blankets, letting them fall on the floor. Then he pulled off the sheets and dragged them back to the chair. Sitting there in the dim light, his hands shaking, he tied the sheets together, corner to corner.

When he was finished, he flung his newly fashioned "rope" across the linoleum floor to see how long it was. It barely stretched beyond his bed. He knew it was too short. What else could he use?

He thought of the fabric shower curtain. He went into the bathroom, reached up and unhooked the plastic clips that suspended the curtain from a rod across the shower.

He dragged the curtain back to the chair. Sitting back down, he picked up the end of the string of sheets and tied it to the corner of the shower curtain. Was it long enough now? It would have to be.

He stepped over to the window and cranked it all the way open. He tied one end of his makeshift rope to the handle and tossed the rest over the ledge.

He stepped back over to the chair and pushed it to the wall beneath the window. Grabbing the back of the chair, he pulled himself up, first kneeling, then standing on the seat.

Holding tight to the marble ledge to steady himself, he swung his right leg over it and stuck it through the open window frame. Then he raised his left leg and extended it behind him too.

He was now on his belly, his head barely still in his room, his legs dangling out of the window. He inched back and grabbed the makeshift rope with both hands. He knew he'd have to climb down quickly, that he couldn't hold on very long. And so he began his descent.

He tried to ignore the throbbing pain in his shoulders, the trembling of his arms, the way the coarse brick wall was digging into his skin. He tried not to look down. He tried not to worry if the rope would be long enough.

Instead, he closed his eyes and breathed in the lilacs and felt the warm breeze on his face and ran down his street to the empty lot and returned to the joy and the freedom of spring.

Rose

"For you," you said, handing me a single red rose.

"Thank you," I said, surprised by your sweet gesture.

I wondered where you'd gotten it. You were just a boy. Did you clip it from your mother's garden?

It didn't matter. That day, I began to fall in love with you.

And every time you gave me a red rose, I fell in love with you again.

Once I said, "We can't afford it."

"Love is priceless," you said.

Every week for 65 years, you gave me a red rose. Every time, I fell in love with you more deeply.

Now I slowly approach you and gently lay a single red rose over your heart.

"For you," I say.

The Strain

They thought they had conquered it, but it came back. It always comes back.

They used science to battle it. They took every measure, used every weapon, developed new weapons. But it would not go away. It kept advancing. It invaded every part of society, from dark alleys to places of worship.

Until then, they considered the virus their most formidable foe. But the virus went away.

Extremism remained. It is still advancing. It is a particularly virulent strain of disease, impervious to both medicine and reason, and as long as it has a willing host, it cannot be eradicated.

I Want to Hold Your Hand

As a kid, I listened to the Beatles sing "I Want to Hold Your Hand" and imagined holding someone's hand like that one day.

Yours was the first hand I held that way. I held it on our first date. I held it at our wedding. I held it as we both held our children's hands too. I held it as we drove to the hospital. I held it when you lay in bed.

I heard that old song again today. I remembered that when I touched you, I felt happy inside.

I want to hold your hand.

Street Ball and Joe's Red Bike

On summer evenings, I used to watch my older brother Joe play football with his buddies in the street. I watched through our bedroom window on the second floor of our house. I was only five, and I wasn't allowed to play football with the older boys, especially in the street.

Theoretically, it was touch football. But it was rough, and someone would always get hurt. Guys would knock heads and skid across the pavement. Someone would trip up the curb or run into a telephone pole or a parked car. Once, Tom Clark tripped over a dog and broke his arm.

It was not uncommon for some parent in our neighborhood to take his or her son to the emergency room because of injuries suffered during those games. One night, Joe broke his collar bone running into a mailbox.

When someone got hurt badly, the moms would insist their sons move their game to the backyards. They would play back there on the grass for a night or two, then find their way back into the street, where injuries would continue to run rampant.

I once asked Joe why they just didn't stay in the backyards.

"Too easy, kid," he said. "Too easy."

I idolized Joe. He was five years older than me. I admired so many things about him. He was smart. He was tall and handsome with wavy blond hair and blue eyes. He played football, basketball, baseball, soccer and hockey. He was a standout in every sport.

But the thing I admired most about Joe is that he was fearless. Nothing seemed to rattle him. I never saw him shrink from a challenge. He was the bravest person I've ever known.

"Life is risk," he would say, then plunge his bike down a hill so steep that the rest of us wouldn't even try to walk down it. Until we saw Joe tear down it on his red Schwinn Phantom, swerving to avoid rocks, bouncing over roots and ruts and narrowly missing trees, then slamming on his brake at the bottom, pumping his fists in the air and yelling, "Come on down, you bastards!" One by one, the rest of us would follow.

All I did was imitate my brother. At first, it wasn't easy. Taking risks didn't come naturally to me. I was okay playing football on the grass.

But the more I watched Joe and the more things I tried, the more I realized what I could do. When Joe became a teenager and pursued new interests, I even took his place leading the pack of footballers in the street.

* * *

I was 13 when Joe enlisted in the Marines. It was 1968.

Dad knew he couldn't talk Joe out of signing up. He tried to persuade him to join the Air Force. But that was like asking Joe to play football on the grass.

"I like the Marines, Dad," he said. "They're brave, and they take good care of each other."

He enlisted in March. Ten days later, he left for basic training. Joe and I said goodbye in the kitchen. Dad was taking him to the train station and, for some reason, I didn't go with them.

"Goodbye, kid," he said, hugging me tightly.

We were not a family that hugged a lot, and it felt strange to feel Joe's body so close to mine. But I loved it. He felt so strong.

"Will you write?" I said.

"Oh, yeah," he said. "And you better write back."

"I will, Joe. I will."

Then he was gone. I remember my mom leaving the kitchen and going upstairs. I heard her bedroom door close, then heard her sobbing. She didn't come out until my father came home.

* * *

I got my first letter from Joe about two weeks later. He said basic training was the hardest thing he'd ever done but he was "getting tough and ready for action."

He wrote me again a couple of times after that. He sounded so confident. It made me imagine him on his bike at the top of that hill, smiling and ready to take the plunge.

I wrote back, proudly telling him I had made the Orioles in Babe Ruth League, the same team he had played on, and that I would be starting at second base, just like him.

In May, he shipped out to a place called Khe Sahn. Fierce battles had been raging there for months. For a while, the Americans were winning, but then the momentum shifted.

This was a strategic base, and the President ordered the military to hold it "at all costs." All branches stepped up, but the Marines were in the vanguard.

On his second day of combat, in a place known as Foxtrot Ridge, Joe's company was ambushed as it moved to support other Marines under fire. Joe was in the front line. He was killed leading the way.

* * *

Joe was my only sibling. As the war raged on, my mother became terrified that I might be drafted. Then, just before I turned 18, the war came to an end.

I was attending an all-boys Catholic high school. On the day the peace accords were signed, Father Laurian asked for volunteers to ring the bell in the church steeple. I was the first to raise my hand.

He recruited 12 of us. He told us to line up single file, up the narrow steps to the belfry, where each of us would pull on the rope for one minute. Twelve minutes for 12 years of US involvement in the war. I made sure I was seventh in line. I wanted to mark the seventh year of the war, 1968, the deadliest year of the war, the year my brother was taken away.

When my turn came, I grabbed the rope and pulled it hard, with all my strength. All I could think of was Joe. I pulled and I pulled and I pulled until Father Laurian grabbed my arm and told me it was time. I gave up the rope and fell to my knees, sobbing, my head at Father Laurian's feet, as the bell continued to toll.

* * *

When I got home that afternoon, I changed clothes, opened the garage door, pulled out Joe's bike and took off down the street.

I rode to the edge of town, to the place where Joe used to take the plunge down the big hill. I stopped and stood up, straddling the bike, and looked over the edge. It was even steeper than I remembered.

I drew a breath, squeezed the hand grips tight and pushed off over the edge. The bike bounced violently on the rocky trail. About 25 yards down, I flew off and landed in some tall grass. Fortunately, I was okay and the bike was too.

I got back on and kept going. Another 50 yards down, the front tire hit a big root. I popped off and landed on my back.

Lying there with the wind knocked out of me, I felt like giving up. But then I heard a voice. "Too easy, kid." I got back on.

Another 50 yards down, I hit a big rut and was tossed off again. This time I flew over the handlebars. I hit the ground hard but rolled. I was okay.

Joe's bike wasn't so lucky, though. The front rim was bent. I rocked it back and forth to test it. It wobbled. But at this point, I was so close. So I got back on and rode the brake the rest of the way. The bike shook badly, but it held up.

I made it. I remembered Joe being in this very spot, pumping his fists in the air. Now I looked up and raised my arms toward heaven.

Then I got off Joe's bike. I walked it over to a patch of grass, laid it down and knelt beside it.

"Goodbye, Joe," I said, touching the sturdy frame one last time.

Joy

The Beauty in Things

Roasted verlasso salmon. Piquillo pepper sauce, broccoli, redskin potatoes, horse radish sour crème. $23.

It was the first entrée that caught his eye on the menu, which was posted on the window. He was trying to cut back on red meat. But he was too hungry to go vegetarian tonight. So salmon sounded perfect. And at $23, he knew he could still have a glass of wine and not bust his expense account. After so many meals on the road, he could do the math in his head.

He pulled open the heavy oak door. The warm air and the scent and sound of sizzling steak drew him inside.

"Welcome to Julian's!" said the hostess.

She sounded cordial, but she wasn't really paying attention.

"Do you have a reservation?" she asked as she busily crossed names off the waiting list.

"Good evening," he said. "No, I don't. Do I need one?"

"No," said the hostess. "I just like to check. Will someone be joining you this evening?"

"No," he said quietly. "Just one."

Finally, she looked up. He was as handsome as he was unassuming. He now had her full attention.

"Very good," she said softly.

He traveled a couple of days a week, almost always alone. But he had never gotten used to sitting at a table by himself. It made him feel awkward.

"Do you serve dinner at the bar?" he asked.

"Yes, of course."

His eyes scanned the restaurant, looking for the bar. But he didn't see one.

"Right this way, sir," said the hostess.

He followed her through the restaurant. The bar was in the back.

They walked by a ladies-night-out table. Several of the women stopped chatting and looked up as he passed. He looked away, as if he didn't notice. But he did notice. He had simply grown used to it.

"Will there be anything else?" the hostess said.

"No. Thank you."

"Enjoy your dinner," she said, lingering for a moment, watching him as he made his way into the bar.

The room was dark and cozy, with just enough space for three tall tables. People were having dinner at two of them. A fire crackled in a stone fireplace, which took up much of one wall. The bar itself was short, with only three stools, all empty. They were the kind with backs, which he liked.

He didn't drink much, but he liked bars. He appreciated their clean lines and vibrant colors. His favorites were the ones where the liquor and wine bottles were carefully arranged on glass shelves and backlit.

This was such a bar. There were two shelves against the back wall. On each was a mosaic of bottles, varied by color and height. He stood back for a moment to take it in, as an art lover might study a painting.

"Good evening, sir," said the bartender. "May I start you out with a drink?"

"Good evening," he said, saddling up to the stool on the right. He was always careful to leave enough space for others.

"Actually," he said, "I'd like to go ahead and order dinner."

"Very good," said the bartender. "Would you like to see a menu?"

"No, thanks. I was looking at your menu outside. I think I'll have the salmon and a glass of your house chardonnay."

"Good choice. Anything else? A cocktail before dinner?"

"No, thanks. But I will take the wine whenever you're ready."

"Very good. Let me place your order, and I'll have your wine in just a moment."

He felt the warmth from the fire on his back and realized he was still wearing his coat. He stood up to take it off, looked around and spotted a coat rack in the corner. He went over to it and hung up his coat.

He was walking back to the bar when he saw someone come in from the restaurant. It was the hostess, followed by a woman.

"Here we are," said the hostess, looking his way. "It looks like we have one open table and, of course, the bar."

"Thank you," said the woman.

The hostess took one last look at him, then disappeared.

He sat back down. He wondered if the woman might come over, but he didn't want to stare. So he took his seat. His glass of wine was waiting.

He took a sip and looked up. Once again, the colorful bottles caught his eye. But now, looking more carefully, he realized there was a large mirror behind them. In it, he could see most of the bar. In the space between the rows of bottles, he could see the reflection of the woman who had just come in.

She was standing in the doorway, looking around the room. She walked to the open table, paused and stepped over to the hearth. She held her hands up to the fire and rubbed them together slowly.

She was tall and thin with long, brown hair. She wore a dark blue coat and a white scarf. He couldn't get a good look at her face. But he guessed she was in her mid-30's, like him.

Watching her in the mirror, he began to feel a bit voyeuristic, so he looked down at his glass of wine. But a few moments later, hearing footsteps behind him, he glanced back up. In the mirror, he saw her approach the stool to his far left.

"Do you mind if I sit here?" she asked.

"No," he said, pivoting slightly to face her. She was quite plain-looking. "Not at all."

"Thanks," she said.

She took off her scarf and coat, then hesitated, not knowing exactly where to put them.

"There's a coat rack in the corner," he said, nodding toward it. He thought about offering to hang up her coat, but that felt too forward.

"Thanks."

He watched her as she walked to the coat rack but faced forward as she turned around to walk back to the bar. She passed behind him and hitched herself up on the stool, leaving one seat between them.

"Good evening, miss," said the bartender. "May I start you out with a drink tonight?"

"Yes," she said, glancing at his wine. "I'd like a glass of your house cabernet, please."

"Certainly. Would you like to see a menu?"

"No, thanks. I saw it out front. I think I'll go ahead and order dinner."

She looked over at him, as if to make sure that would be okay.

"By all means," he said. "I've just ordered dinner myself."

"Then I'd like the filet mignon," she said, "medium rare, with a baked potato and mixed vegetables."

"Sour cream?"

"Yes, please."

"Very good," he said. "I'll be right back with your wine, miss, and some fresh bread for each of you."

Fresh bread. Please hurry, he thought. After hearing "filet mignon," he was suddenly feeling famished — and a little wimpy for ordering the salmon.

He turned to her.

"My name is Michael," he said, smiling and extending his hand.

"Hello," she said. "I'm Sarah."

Her hand was thin, but her grip was surprisingly strong. She held his hand tightly and didn't let go right away, causing him to face her a moment longer. He looked into her face. It was as plain as winter wheat. But not for long because her eyes, which sparkled like emeralds, lit it up. They made it lovely. It was as if her face were a blank canvas on which some unseen artist has begun to work.

The part of him which did not like to stare gave way to the part which was drawn to the beauty in the most ordinary things. And so, for a moment, he looked into her eyes. He could not avert his gaze. Nor did he want to.

Nor could she take her eyes off of him. She had never seen such a good-looking man, at least not in person. His skin was olive. His eyes were blue. His jaw was strong. His cheeks and chin were covered with stubble. His black hair, combed back, fell down to his shoulders, curling at his neck. She wondered if he was a model.

"Here you are, miss," said the bartender, setting down her glass of wine. "Enjoy."

And with that, at last, she released her grip. He let go too, and they both swiveled back toward the bar.

"Cheers," he said, raising his glass.

"Cheers," she said, grateful for the opportunity to see his face again.

She watched him take a drink. He was not wearing a ring.

"So what brings you here?" he asked.

"Business," she said. "I'm here on business."

"Me too."

"I'm visiting customers."

"So am I."

"What do you do?" she asked.

"I'm sort of in the furniture business."

"Sort of?" she asked with a smile.

"Well, yes. I'm in the office furniture business."

Office furniture? Now she wasn't sure if she was more curious or less. He sensed her hesitation.

"I'm a designer. I work with high-end clients to design executive offices."

"Sounds interesting," she said, sounding relieved.

"It is, most of the time."

"Most of the time?"

"Well," he said, "when my clients let me design."

This time, she didn't ask for clarification. She simply smiled and tilted her head, as if to say go on.

"I mean my clients are very successful," he said. "But they're business people. They're not designers. That's where I come in. When they let me design, when they take me seriously, I do my best work."

He looked down at his wine glass, squeezing the stem between his fingertips. *What am I doing? All she did was ask me what I do.*

"When they take you seriously?" she said.

"Yeah."

"Why wouldn't your clients take you seriously?"

"Some people," he said, deciding to roll with it, "tend to judge a book by its cover."

"What do you mean?"

"Some of my customers, at least at first, see me as a lightweight."

"A lightweight?"

"A pretty boy."

That's understandable, she thought. But she simply said, "Oh."

"They're wrong, of course," he said. He didn't mean to sound so defensive. "I mean they're mistaken about me being a lightweight."

"How do you convince them you're not?"

He looked up to see if she was really interested. He couldn't tell. But then again, he could never tell for sure.

"Through my work," he said. "I show them what I can do."

"I see."

"Dinner is served," said the bartender, returning with both their plates. He set hers down, then his. Michael looked at his salmon, then over at her steak. *I really need to get off this diet.*

"What about you?" he said. "What do you do?"

"I'm an IT specialist. Essentially, I'm a troubleshooter. My company sends me out to help customers solve big computer problems, the ones we can't handle over the phone or online."

"So, do you travel a lot?"

"Yeah, a lot," she said. "Too much really."

"You don't like to travel?"

"It's okay. It's just that ..."

"What?"

"It's just that I really like working with computers, but I'm not crazy about working with people."

Now it was his turn to simply smile and tilt his head.

"I love math," she said. "That's how I got into computers."

"That's cool. What is it you love about math?"

She paused, wondering how much to share. She wasn't sure if this perfect stranger was all that interested. But he did ask. It would be impolite not to answer.

“Some people are put off by math," she said. “But I’ve always loved numbers. I know it might sound crazy, but there is something about numbers that I find very appealing."

He must think I’m such a geek.

“What do you think that is?” he asked.

“I’m not sure. But I think it has something to do with being so authentic."

"So authentic?"

“I mean numbers are just what they are. A four is a four. It will never be a five. And it makes no apologies for being a four."

He grinned.

"Well," she said. "It's as unapologetic as a number can be."

He laughed. His laugh was even deeper, but softer, than she had imagined.

"I like numbers because they're real,” she said. "They’re solid. You can rely on them. And I'm drawn to that."

“You mean you can count on them?”

His pun caught her by surprise. She laughed loudly, and watching her laugh made him laugh too.

“So how did you get into computers?”

“Well, for a while, I thought about teaching math,” she said. “I even did some tutoring in college. But I’m just not very good with people. So I went into computers. That way I thought I could focus on math and not have worry too much about people. But as it turns out, working with people is now a big part of my job.”

“If you don’t mind me asking,” he said, “why don’t you like working with people?”

"I like people," she said. "But to most people I work with, I'm just a computer geek. I'm there to fix their problems. And then I move on, and I never hear from them again. After a while, it makes you feel like just another part of the service contract."

"I see," he said. "I'm sorry."

Oh no. Now I've made this guy feel sorry for me.

Suddenly, she felt she'd shared too much. She felt awkward. She felt like getting up and walking away.

"Thank you for sharing that," he said. "I know exactly what you mean."

His kindness took her breath away.

"You do?"

"Yeah. All my life, I've felt people were looking past me. They see me on the outside, and they form conclusions. But hardly anyone takes the time to get to know me. I mean the real me. No one ever asks me what I think."

"I know what you mean."

"You do?"

"Yes, I do," she said, "because no one ever asks me how I feel."

For a moment, they sat in silence.

"It kind of makes you feel one-dimensional, doesn't it?" he said.

"Yeah. That's a good way to put it."

"But the good news," he said, trying to lighten things up again, "is that you found a way to do what you love. Math, I mean."

"Yeah," she said, smiling. "I guess you're right. I do get to work with numbers every day."

"How is your food, folks?" asked the bartender.

They looked down at their plates and realized they hadn't eaten much.

"Good," Michael lied. His salmon was as bland as tapioca.

"You've barely touched your salmon," the bartender said to him. "Is it okay?"

"It's fine. But next time," he said with a smile, "I'm going with the filet."

"Would you like me to exchange it?"

"No, thanks," Michael said. "But I'd love another glass of wine. How about you, Sarah?"

"Sure," she said.

He looked over at her. She was cutting into her filet. She sliced off a big piece and speared it with her fork. And with a newfound boldness, she reached across the bar, held the meat between them and looked up at him and said, "Please take some of mine. I could never eat it all anyway."

He smiled.

"Thank you," he said, instinctively picking up his plate and setting it down between them. He noticed her hand was shaking. He placed his left hand on hers and, with his right, slid the beef off of her fork and onto his plate. Her hand was still shaking, and he held it for an extra moment.

"Will you make mine a cab too?" he called to the bartender.

"Of course."

"So tell me, Sarah," Michael said, eagerly cutting into the filet. "Have you always loved math?"

"Always," she said, "even as a girl. Of course, that didn't make me very popular. None of the other girls cared much for math, and boys don't tend to go crazy over math geeks, especially when they're about a foot taller."

He smiled.

"But you stuck with it."

"Yeah, I stuck with it."

"And I'm sure the boys eventually came around."

“Not really,” she said, wondering again if she was being too open.

“Oh, come on. Surely you had guys after you.”

“Not one," she said, shaking her head.

“You mean you never dated in school?”

"What I'm telling you is that I've never had a date."

Good lord. I can’t believe I just said that.

He looked over at her to make sure she wasn’t kidding. A certain sadness in her face told him she was telling the truth.

"There are a lot of good guys out there,” he said.

"Yeah, there are, and I've been interested in some of them. But none has been interested in me."

The bartender was back with their wine.

“May I take your plates?"

"Sure," Michael said.

"Yes, please," Sarah said.

"Will there be anything else right now?"

"No, thanks," they said in unison. The bartender took the hint and retreated to the kitchen.

"You just haven't met the right guy yet," Michael said quietly. "I mean somebody who can see the real you."

She looked at him and smiled. He was so sweet. She took a sip of wine. Her mind tended to work in metrics, and she pondered the long odds of this night.

“What about you?” she said. “Tell me about you."

"What would you like to know?"

"Tell me why a designer is in the office furniture business.”

He took a sip of wine.

"You really want to know?"

"Are you kidding? I just told you I'm a math geek and I've never had a date. Bring it on."

He chuckled.

“When I was a kid, I wanted to be an artist. I guess my parents spotted some talent in me because, when I was only six, they signed me up for art lessons and bought me a bunch of art supplies. They even set up a little studio for me in our den. I used to spend hours and hours drawing and painting in there."

"What did you draw?"

"Well, I pretty much drew the everyday things around me — a chair, a desk, a TV, a lamp, a filing cabinet, books on bookshelves. I even drew my sister, my brother and my dog, although none of them would sit very still."

She laughed at the thought of his dog sitting for a portrait. He was glad to know she was still paying attention.

"We had a long, sliding glass window with a thin marble sill in that room," he said. "My mother put five crystal decanters along the sill. She filled them with water and added a few drops of food coloring. Red, green, blue, yellow and purple. When the sunlight streamed in through the window, they looked like a rainbow. I sat there and looked at those decanters and the way the light came through them for hours. And I painted them dozens of times. They were my favorite things to paint. And they were always a challenge because the light and the colors were always changing."

"That sounds so lovely," she said.

"Well, that's just it. My art teacher had a very different idea of beauty. She wanted me to do mountains and sunsets and windmills. But to me, the ordinary things around me were the real things of beauty, the true objects of art."

"So what did you do?"

"Well, my teacher was pretty stubborn — and persuasive. She convinced my parents I should 'broaden my horizons.' So I began drawing mountain ranges and windmills, things I'd never even seen."

"Did you like it?"

"No! I hated it. But I did it. I painted those things for my teacher and my parents. But I kept painting desks and chairs and those decanters too. I hid that work in a big box I kept in my closet."

"Did your parents ever find out?"

"No. They had no clue. In fact, they were so thrilled with my landscapes that they sent me to art school for college."

"How was that?"

"Initially, awful. But over time, great because I got exposed to interior design, which I loved. When I graduated, I went to work designing offices."

"So you stuck with it too?"

"Yeah," he said. "Except for that little side trip to learn how to draw mountains."

"You found a way to do what you've always loved," she said.

"Yeah."

He looked up at the bottles on the shelves behind the bar. The colors sparkled in the reflection of the flicker of the flames from the fireplace.

Then he looked back over at her. The fire danced in her eyes. Now, though, they weren't just green. Now they were alive with the color from every bottle. And suddenly her face, though still plain, looked so very elegant. It was transformed, not by the bottles or even her eyes, but by a light that came from inside.

He drew a breath and blinked.

"Sarah?"

"Yeah?"

"Have you ever had your portrait painted?"

She paused, thinking he was kidding. But then she looked at his face and saw he was waiting for an answer.

"No," she said. "I haven't."

"Would you be open to it?"

"Yeah, I guess."

"Are you still in town tomorrow evening?"

"Yes."

"Great. Then let's get together tomorrow. I'll bring my sketch book."

"Really?"

"Yeah, really," he said, smiling and raising his glass. "It's a date."

Sun

I look out this window every morning. It's usually still dark when I get up and sit here with my coffee.

I like to watch the sun rise. I can't actually see the sun from where I sit, but it doesn't matter. I see clouds appear in the bright sky. I see trees — green, red and purple — shimmer in a light from the East.

The trees and clouds were here when I awoke, and they'll be here tonight when darkness falls. I won't see them, but I'll know they're here because of the light of a sun I don't see.

One Floor Up

It began in an elevator.

It was just after noon on a Wednesday. I was on my way to the cafeteria. It was only three floors up. Normally, I would've taken the stairs. But I was in a hurry, just grabbing a sandwich to eat at my desk.

The elevator stopped at eight. You were standing there alone, holding a book.

"Ten, please," you said softly, as you stepped inside. As you turned around, you saw the button was already lit. "Never mind," you added with a small laugh.

You were standing right in front of me. Under the bright ceiling lights, I noticed some red and a few strands of gray in your chestnut brown hair.

The doors opened at nine. Several more people got in. You stepped back, and your left heel came down hard on the toe of my left shoe.

“Uggh!”

You wheeled around.

“Oh, I’m so sorry!”

Turning around that way just as the elevator started ascending again threw you off balance. Instinctively, I grabbed your upper arms from behind and steadied you.

"It's OK," I said. “I’m fine.”

You faced forward and said nothing. I imagined you were embarrassed.

The doors opened, and everyone got out. I made my way to the deli station and ordered salami on rye. I looked around and saw you heading to the salad bar.

As I stood in line, I watched you place a plate, silverware, a napkin and your book on a tray and make your salad. You were wearing low heel pumps. No wonder my left foot was throbbing.

You stepped over to the drink station. I noticed your toned calf muscles and slender waist. You dispensed Diet Pepsi into a tall glass.

You got in line for the cashier. You paid, stopped for salad dressing and walked into the dining room alone.

I grabbed my sandwich and a drink and headed back to my office. As the elevator passed the eighth floor, I wondered if you work there.

* * *

You were at least 10 years my senior, but I couldn’t stop thinking about you. I wanted to see you again.

I wondered if you went to the cafeteria for lunch every day. I took a chance. Just after noon the next day, I got on the elevator. It stopped at eight, and there you were.

Once again, you were holding a book. Once again, you stood right in front of me. And once again, the doors opened at nine, and several more people got in.

This time, you were careful to avoid my toes. But a big guy backed into you, pushing you against me and forcing me against the back wall. Instinctively, I put my hands on the sides of your waist to keep you from pressing into me.

"I'm sorry," I said.

"It's okay," you said, lightly taking hold of my left hand. "You probably kept me from stepping on your other foot."

Your hair smelled like flowers. I looked down at your left hand and noticed you weren't wearing a ring.

The doors opened at 10. Everyone got out. You glanced over your shoulder, smiled and said, "Thank you again." Your eyes were honey-brown.

"You're welcome," I said.

I waited in line for a sandwich and watched as you once again got a salad and walked into the dining room alone.

* * *

It was Friday. Everyone in my office dresses down on Friday. Some even wear jeans. But today I wore a suit.

All morning, I watched the clock. I couldn't wait for lunchtime. Just after noon, I got into the elevator. I prayed that the doors would open at eight.

They did. And there you were!

Today you were wearing a sleeveless, red dress and holding a small, silver purse. You were looking at the spot where I always stand. When you saw me, you smiled.

"Hello again," you said.

"Hello," I said, smiling back.

This time, you stepped in and pivoted just before you got to me, your back against the outside wall. We were at right angles. You glanced up at my face. I held your gaze for a moment. Then you looked down.

I couldn't take my eyes off your dress.

As everyone was filing out, you turned to me and said, "Have a good weekend."

"You too."

I watched you walk away. Your step, like your body, was lithe.

Waiting for my sandwich, I watched you disappear into the dining room. This time, I followed you.

You were sitting alone at a table next to a window. In the sunlight, you looked older and even lovelier.

You smiled as I approached.

"Would you like some company?" I said.

"I'd love some."

Your Card

It had been a hard winter, harder than any winter I could remember. Wet and gray, virus-infected, closed-off, hushed, shot through with loss. No one came by. The whole world felt hollow. Even the streets were empty.

Then one day I got your card. "Just checking in," you wrote. Simple as that.

It was just a card. But I wasn't expecting anything. I had lowered my expectations.

Now I'm looking out my window, thinking of you. It's early evening, but it's still light out. I've noticed it's been staying light longer lately. I have so missed the light.

Free

As a senior in high school, Brian Quinn quietly had a thing for a pretty girl named Hannah, even though his friend Jack Kelly was her boyfriend. One day, Brian stepped over to Hannah's locker and asked her out. He assumed she'd say no. He was shocked when she said yes.

When Jack found out, he was devastated. One day, he didn't show up at school. That evening, Brian learned that Jack was in the hospital. He'd slit his wrists.

Brian blamed himself. He wanted to visit Jack but felt too guilty.

Jack never came back to school. He was admitted to a psychiatric hospital. Brian couldn't bring himself to visit. He was still too filled with guilt.

That fall, Brian left for college. He had nightmares about Jack. He couldn't sleep. He began missing classes. His grades slipped. He started drinking.

After his freshman year, Brian dropped out of school and got a job on a construction crew. That summer, he heard that Jack was leaving for college out of state in the fall.

Once he'd left for college, Jack didn't come back to town much. Brian never left. He never went back to college. He never got married. For the next 40 years, he worked on construction crews.

After college, Jack moved to Minneapolis, where he joined a restaurant group as a market analyst. Jack was bright and hard-working. He rose through the ranks and, at 47, became CEO.

* * *

Nearly 50 years after Brian had graduated from high school, late one night, his car was hit by a truck. Brian had crossed the centerline.

Three days later, he woke up in the hospital.

"You're awake," someone said.

"Who's there?"

Brian heard the footsteps of someone approaching his bed. He looked up and saw a man he assumed was a doctor.

"What happened?" Brian said.

"You were in an accident."

"How bad?"

"You'll be here for a while. But you'll live."

Brian noticed the man at his bedside wasn't wearing white.

"Who are you?"

"Don't you remember me? I'm Jack Kelly."

Brian felt his heart skip a beat. It was Jack! Brian began to cry.

Jack took hold of Brian's bandaged hand.

"It's okay," he said.

Once Brian had composed himself, he looked up and said, "I'm sorry."

"For what?" Jack said.

"For taking Hannah away. For causing you to almost take your own life."

"Oh, Brian. You didn't cause that. I was mentally ill. Cutting myself was a cry for help. After that, I finally got the help I needed."

"But you're so successful."

"Yes, but that's only because I've had lots of help," Jack said. "I decided to help others too. I made addressing mental illness our corporate cause. Did you know that?"

Brian shook his head.

"Yeah. We've made a big difference, and it wouldn't have happened without you. I'm only sorry it's taken me so long to thank you. When I heard about your accident, I came right away, hoping I wasn't too late."

Montage

When he was a kid, Jeremy loved to paint by number. He worked hard to match colors and numbers and stay inside the lines. As a result, his paintings looked just like the stylized images on the covers of his paint kits.

One day, Jeremy came home from school upset from a scolding by his teacher. He was a sensitive boy, and the scene in front of his classmates had brought him to tears.

Jeremy went up to his room and began to paint, not sure of what else to do. But he was still so upset that his hand was shaking. He was lost in his thoughts. He couldn't stay inside the lines.

When he was finished, he stepped back from his work, a mountain scene, and examined it. It looked unlike anything he had ever painted. Not only were the edges of the colors uneven, some of the colors themselves were clearly wrong. Blue snow on a mountaintop, orange pine trees, green water.

Seeing this, Jeremy became even more distressed. He had always been proud to show off his paintings, but he felt like throwing this one away.

Just then, his mother came in. She saw tears.

"What's wrong, honey?"

"I messed it all up."

"What?"

"My painting."

"Oh, honey," she said, putting her arms around him. "It's okay."

"No, it's not!" he said, pushing her away. "It's terrible."

"Let me see."

She stepped over to his table and had a look.

"Oh, Jeremy! It's beautiful. I love what you've done here. This might be my favorite of your paintings yet."

"How can you say that?" Jeremy whimpered. "Can't you see where I messed up? It doesn't look anything like the picture on the box."

"No, it doesn't. It's you. That's what makes it so beautiful."

"Really?" Jeremy said, wiping his eyes. "You really like it?"

"I love it. And I can't wait to show Dad when he gets home."

Jeremy's father liked it too.

"You're becoming a real artist," he said.

After that, Jeremy switched from painting by number to painting with watercolors on white sheets of paper. He didn't sketch anything. He just started painting, either random shapes and colors or certain images in his mind. He liked these paintings and the act of creating them so much more.

Seeing the joy this new type of painting brought Jeremy, his mother bought him a framed canvas and an easel. Jeremy stood and painted a hillside covered with flowers of various shapes and colors. He had never seen such a hillside. He'd simply imagined it.

Soon Jeremy was painting on large sheets of canvas on the floor of his garage. He no longer painted the images in his head, though. Now he tried to express the emotions in his heart.

He dashed red rage this way and blue serenity that way, swept green hope here and grey frustration there and drizzled everything with yellow happiness. Jeremy's paintings were a montage of the emotions he was feeling in his life.

In time, his paintings sold for thousands at auction. People said they spoke to them.

Doing the Dishes

They were busy professionals. Most days, they barely saw each other. Their marriage felt the strain. Every little thing seemed to be a big deal anymore.

So they were really upset when their dishwasher broke and they learned the repair service couldn't get to it for two weeks.

At first, they took turns taking care of the dishes. Then one Sunday, a rare day off for both of them, they decided he would wash and she would dry.

They began talking and listening in a way they hadn't in a long time. The next day, he called the repair service and canceled their order.

Conversion

Jim didn't like being the equipment manager for his high school baseball team. Guys called him "geek." Girls ignored him. Jim loved baseball, but he wasn't quite good enough to make the team. He signed on as equipment manager just to be near the action.

Late one afternoon, after a pre-season practice, Jim heard someone yell "Stop!" It was a girl's voice, coming from the bleachers.

Jim was putting equipment away. Everyone else had gone. He looked over and saw two girls and two guys standing at the base of the bleachers.

"I said stop!"

Jim saw one of the girls slap one of the guys. Both guys laughed.

"Help!" she yelled.

Jim ran toward them. By the time he got there, one of the guys had grabbed one of the girls by her arm.

"Get away from me!" she cried.

"What's going on here?" Jim said.

"None of your business, geek," said one of the guys.

"We were just having some fun," said the other, as the girl wriggled free from him.

"Bullshit!" she said.

"I think you better leave," said Jim.

"Says who?" said the bigger of the two guys.

Jim stepped toward him and, without hesitating, slugged him in the jaw. He dropped straight to the ground.

The other guy came at Jim, but just as he was about to take a swing, the girls started screaming so loudly that he covered his ears and ran away.

Then the girls shouted "Thank you!" as they too ran off.

"Thank you!" Jim called after them.

Jim went back to the trailer, where he'd been putting equipment away. He figured if the guy he decked came after him, he'd grab a bat. But he slunk off.

Word got out about the incident around school. Kids stopped calling Jim geek. When several players got injured that spring, the coach invited Jim to join the team. Right after that, a girl asked him to prom.

And the girls who drove away the guy who was about to hit Jim formed an after-school self-defense class.

Merry Christmas

I see him every morning, standing at the corner, holding a cardboard sign. The light there changes so fast that he usually makes it only to the first car stopped. I always hang back.

But I feel bad for him in his ragged clothes. As the temperature drops, I worry about him.

Lately he's been wearing a Santa hat. This morning, I pulled up to the light and rolled down my window.

"Merry Christmas, sir!" he said.

"Good morning," I said, handing him my winter coat.

He looked at the coat, and his eyes grew wide.

"Thank you!" he said, flashing a gap-toothed smile.

I looked up. The light had changed.

"Merry Christmas," I said, pulling away.

The Red Wagon

When he was a boy, he had a red wagon. His earliest memories are of his mother pulling him down the sidewalk.

He remembers his mother giving him a box of animal crackers for the ride. He remembers the little thump caused by each seam of the sidewalk. He remembers coming home, where his mother would give him a glass of cold milk.

Now his life is hard. But on his toughest days, when he might go mad, he closes his eyes and holds on to the sides of his red wagon, feeling the bumps of the sidewalk and going home again.

About the Author

After a long career in the corporate world, Don Tassone has returned to his creative writing roots.

Collected Stories is his eighth book. The others are the novels *Francesca* and *Drive* and the short story collections *Snapshots, New Twists, Sampler, Small Bites* and *Get Back.*

Don and his wife Liz live in Loveland, Ohio. They have four children and nine grandchildren.

Visit Don at dontassone.com.

www.ingramcontent.com/pod-product-compliance
Lightning Source LLC
Chambersburg PA
CBHW070554120726
47909CB00007B/2341

* 9 7 8 0 5 7 8 3 5 4 3 5 4 *